THE BEDROOM IS Mine

JANE BONANDER

THE BEDROOM IS MINE
Copyright © 2023 by Jane Bonander

ISBN: 979-8-88653-235-7

Published by Satin Romance
An Imprint of Melange Books, LLC
White Bear Lake, MN 55110
www.satinromance.com

Published in the United States of America.

Cover Design by Ashley Redbird Designs

In memory of my parents,
Floyd and Mabel Olson

Prologue

Twin Hearts, California
New Year's Eve, 1879

Tugging mercilessly at his stiff collar, Ross spat out a vile oath, then strangled the urge to swear again. He hated getting trussed up like a turkey. Might as well put a damned noose around his neck and hang him from the nearest tree. One was as uncomfortable as the other.

He pulled cold air into his lungs, savoring it. And savoring the brief quiet. Except for the distant burbling of the river caressing the rocks as it made its way south, there was no sound he wanted to hear. He let the river sounds soothe him as he tried to block the noise that filtered out from inside his sister and brother-in-law's house.

His dog, the faithful lab mix Red, curled up at his feet, Ross leaned against the porch railing and closed his eyes. He thought about Trudy and how much he wanted to slip into her warm bed and between her lusty white thighs. He swore again, getting hard just thinking about it.

He took a long, angry pull on his cigarette as he stood in the shadows, listening to the shallow laughter of those inside as they prepared to ring in the New Year.

He called himself ten kinds of a fool for letting Samantha drag him to one of her shindigs again. Unfortunately, his younger sister could wrap him around her little finger, and she knew it.

The back door opened, allowing a stream of light to wash across the porch and Red lifted his huge head off the floor to see who intruded on his nap time.

"Ross Benedict, are you hiding out here?" The voice was filled with pique.

"You know damned good and well I'm hiding out here, Sam." Ross flicked away the cigarette he'd been smoking, the ash dying the moment it hit the damp grass.

She shut the door behind her and before pulling her shawl around her shoulders, she reached down and gave Red a head scratch. "Aletha Carmody is looking everywhere for you."

He didn't like the teasing tone of her voice. "Aletha Carmody has a face that would stop a clock and a voice that scares my dog."

Sam sputtered an exasperated sound. "Oh, I thought she'd be perfect for you. Really, I did."

Reaching into his pocket, Ross dragged out his tobacco pouch and a piece of paper. As he rolled himself another cigarette, he retorted, "Just like you thought Olive Hornsby would be perfect for me last year? And Hortense Cobb the year before that?"

Samantha sighed. "Olive Hornsby married Elias Rhodes last May, Ross. They're expecting a baby sometime after the first of the year. That could have been *you*."

He lit his cigarette and visibly shuddered at the thought of bedding the scrawny, pale Olive Hornsby. "Well, thank the bloody hell it wasn't." He took a drag on the cigarette, then stamped it out beneath his boot—perhaps a bit harder than was necessary. He could feel Sam's eyes probe him through the darkness.

"All I want is for you to be as happy as I am."

There was a wistfulness in her voice that he forced himself to ignore. It wasn't...*natural* for a man to tie himself down to one woman. He didn't understand how men did it. Of course, if he ever discovered that Derek, his brother-in-law, had cheated on Sam, he'd twist the man's balls until they came off in his hand, then make him eat them.

"And the only way I can possibly be happy is to be married?" He was incredulous. After all these years, she still didn't get it. He loved the bachelor life.

"Well, of course." Her voice had the ring of false innocence to it. She nodded toward the door. "Aletha is probably wondering if you've skedaddled back to your cabin in the woods."

Ross snorted. "If she's thinking that, she's smarter than I've given her credit for. And speaking of the cabin, Sam, when are you going to let me buy you out?"

She brushed her hand across his shoulder. "Not any time soon. And I refuse to talk business on New Year's Eve. Once I sell you my share, I'll have nothing left of Mama and Papa's."

He smiled in the darkness, sensing her sadness. Although she was a married woman, she was still his little sister. "It's not as if someone you don't know is living there, Sam."

"I know. I know. Oh," she wailed on a soft sigh, "I don't want to be sad tonight. We're having a party. Come." She tugged on his arm. "Aletha is waiting for you."

He cursed again, resisting her pull. "She spent the entire

3

night hanging on my arm, tittering and giggling like a dull-witted child. How in God's name do you expect me to put up with something like that? And the *questions*. Hell, Sam, she bombarded me with questions. 'Do you like children, Ross? You'd be such a wonderful father,'" he mimicked in a simpering voice. "'Do you like cherry tarts, Ross? Why, I make the best cherry tarts in Twin Hearts.' And she kept squeezing my arm, saying, 'My, my, aren't you the strong one? I'll just bet you could lift little ol' me up with one hand. Oh, but that beard.'" He clucked foolishly. "'Doesn't all that facial hair bother you, Ross?' Then she lets out this godawful whinnying giggle. It grates on me like a saw on an anvil. Besides," he groused, "I like my beard."

Samantha laughed quietly beside him. "You mean you wouldn't shave off your mustache and beard for a very special woman?"

"Hell would freeze over before I did." He'd grown accustomed to his beard and would feel naked without it. He suddenly felt her eyes questioning him through the darkness. "What is it?"

"How about a little friendly wager, brother dear?"

"Like what?" he asked, skeptical.

"I'll bet that if the right woman came along and asked you to shave, you'd do it."

He didn't like the sound of that. "Gambling isn't ladylike, Sam."

"Afraid you'll lose?"

He sensed her cocky, self-assured smile. "Hell, no, and I'll prove it. Name the terms."

"I'll bet you…" She paused and tugged at his beard. "I'll bet that a year from now, you'll have no beard or mustache, and it will be because of a woman." She sounded ridiculously triumphant.

4

"And if it doesn't happen?"

"Well," she began, "then I promise on a stack of Bibles that I won't ever try to marry you off again."

He guffawed, unable to help himself. "You couldn't stop meddling in my life if your own depended on it."

"I'm serious, Ross. Cross my heart."

"Yeah, I know. You cross your heart with one hand, and the other is behind your back with its fingers crossed."

"Oh, don't be gutless, you big boob. Do we have a deal or not?"

He chuckled at her persistence. "Sure. Hell, why not?

The door opened, and Derek stepped onto the porch. "What are you two doing out here? Ross, Aletha Carmody is looking everywhere for you. And Samantha," he added, pulling his wife into his arms, "it's almost midnight. My arms are empty without you. I don't want to miss my New Year's kiss."

"Oh, dear heart," she said, her voice filled with love, "you can kiss me anytime and all the time."

"But we had our first kiss on New Year's Eve, sweet lips, and I plan on kissing you on this night every year for the rest of our lives."

Ross would have gagged had the man not been his brother-in-law. Christ! Did men really talk this way to women?

"Oh, all right, you silly goose. Anyway, I've missed you too, and I'm cold." She cuddled against him and waited for him to open the door.

"Come along, brother, dear," she called over her shoulder. "Althea is waiting for you." Her voice was filled with gentle mocking.

Ross grunted. He looked at Red, who was watching him. "If I were you, I'd stay outside." Then with great reluctance, he turned to follow Sam inside, feeling the lamb being led to the slaughter. Never again, damnit. Never again! This was the last

5

time he'd ever let Samantha set him up. Hell, he liked his life just the way it was. Responsible to no one but himself. He neither wanted nor needed some damned woman trying to fit him into her own personal little mold. Crowding his space. Constantly cleaning and bustling around the cabin, complaining of his propensity for mess. He shuddered at the thought.

Next year would be different. Sam's little New Year's Eve party would occur without him. If she tried to wiggle out of her promise not to meddle again, he'd just ignore her and the women she threw at him. He resolved never to let her interfere in his life again.

Aletha Carmody's titter scratched against his ears, and he flinched. Swallowing another curse, he took a deep, resigned breath and dragged himself into the house.

Chapter One

October 1880

Rain came down in buckets, rare shards of lightning cut through the night sky, followed by rumbling thunder.

Lily thanked the driver for the ride, then struggled out of the wagon, drawing her valise beneath her slicker to keep it dry. She watched the wagon lumber on, wondering how the poor horses could pull it through the mud. She'd been grateful for the ride, although she'd hoped to get farther than this. It had taken the better part of a week to get from San Francisco to this place, whatever and wherever it was. She was still near the coast; she often heard the crashing of the waves as they hit the rocks, and the air, though now filled with rain, still held the tang of salt.

Everything she knew and now feared was behind her, and she had given herself enough time to make sure she wouldn't be followed.

Lightning flashed again, allowing her to read the sign on the outskirts of the town. Twin Hearts. In a futile gesture, she picked up her wet, muddy skirt and slogged through the muck, hoping to find some shelter from the storm.

By morning, Lily was cold and miserable to the bone. She'd discovered refuge under a rickety lean-to on the edge of town and her companion for the night was a scraggly cat who found the shelter first but allowed Lily to share it. Now said cat was curled into a ball and pressed tightly against Lily's legs for warmth.

The rain had stopped, but the sky was still a dull slate gray, and the air was wet. Lily knew California weather well enough to know that it was only a brief reprieve.

She nudged the cat off her skirt, pulled off the slicker and shook it, sending sprays of water into the damp air. From her knees down, her skirt and petticoats were sodden and streaked with mud. Inside her shoes, her toes squished against the wet soles. She touched her hair and cringed; the tight curls were matted to her head.

Pulling in a cleansing breath, she straightened and looked around. Perhaps a few hundred yards beyond her was the main street of Twin Hearts. It was there that she would look for a job. The rancher who had given her a ride this far had told her there was a lumber mill outside of town. She hoped they needed a cook.

She glanced down at her clothes and her heart sank. How would she find a job looking like a rain-soaked, filthy urchin?

There was a brief break in the clouds, sending sunshine spraying through the watery air. A rainbow shone vividly against the green-spattered hills, the sight so lovely Lily's breath snagged in her throat.

Behind her, she heard the creak of a buggy. She turned to watch as it rocked toward her, feeling a sense of cautious surprise when it stopped beside her.

A young woman in a fur-trimmed bonnet poked her head out of the buggy window. "Good morning!" She had one of those rare friendly smiles that lit up an already pretty face.

Lily swallowed and wiped her hands nervously against her dress. "Good morning," she answered.

"You're new around here, aren't you?"

Lily couldn't help but laugh. "Just arrived last night." By hitching rides and walking and sleeping under trees, she thought but didn't add. She was fortunate enough to have an innate sense of self-preservation, and she'd never accepted a ride from a man who was alone, no matter how harmless he appeared. The man who had given her a ride as far as Twin Hearts had had two young children with him. When she'd slept in barns, she was gone before dawn. All in all, her trip from San Francisco, though an adventure, had been without incident.

"Where are you from?"

"San Francisco," Lily answered after a short pause. An address more specific wasn't necessary.

The woman chewed at her lower lip, then narrowed her gaze at Lily. "You must be wet and cold."

"I most certainly am." Lily had never been one to mince words.

The young woman continued to stare at her. "I had my driver stop because I was nearly blinded by your wonderful coppery hair. It catches the sunlight like a bright new penny."

Lily laughed again. "How very poetic! And a nice way of saying that my hair's so bright I could lead miners into a mine shaft without a lamp."

The woman merely smiled. A strange, secretive smile. "My name is Samantha Browne."

It was all so ridiculous. Two women conversing like they'd just met at a little soiree in San Francisco, nibbling finger sandwiches and drinking tea. "Lily Sawyer."

"Nice to meet you, Lily Sawyer. Get your things and come with me."

The invitation took Lily by surprise, and she stepped back. "I beg your pardon?"

"Surely you'd like to dry out a bit."

Lily swallowed a jaded retort. The woman was probably from the local bawdy house. She thought about it, aching for a chance to dry out. Maybe even have a bath. And a hot meal. Saliva pooled around her tongue at the thought of food. Bawdy house or not, she couldn't turn the offer down.

"Samantha Browne," Lily began, "you must be my guardian angel." Draping her slicker over her arm, she picked up her damp valise and stepped through the mud to the buggy.

She paused and glanced back at the lean to, wondering about the cat.

"Is something wrong?" the young woman asked.

"Well," Lily began, "I had a feline bed partner last night, and I hate to leave her…"

"You have a cat? Well, of course, poor thing. Bring it along."

Lily sighed. "It isn't my cat. It was here when I arrived."

The young woman, Samantha, left the carriage and strode purposely to the lean to and stepped inside. She returned with the critter tucked close to her chest, apparently unaware that the cat was filthy, leaving dirt on her beautiful coat.

"We can't leave it here," she announced.

"But…I don't even have a place to stay yet. I'm sure I'll find something in town, but would they let me keep a cat?"

Her driver, a young man with the sprouting of a mustache, jumped down and put Lily's belongings on the seat beside him.

As the carriage moved forward, Samantha placed her gloved hand over Lily's work worn one. "Let's worry about one thing at a time."

~

The house was lovely. And it wasn't a bawdy house but the home of Samantha Browne and her husband, Derek, who ran the logging firm on the far side of Twin Hearts.

Lily sat by the fire, wrapped in one of Samantha's plush, warm robes. She combed her fingers through her hair, fluffing it occasionally to help it dry. She felt like royalty; never in her life had she been treated so well.

She'd been informed that the cat was in the kitchen near the stove, slurping up a saucer of milk.

Samantha entered the room from the kitchen carrying a tray of coffee and scones, still warm from the oven. She placed it on the large round table in front of the couch, then glanced at Lily, obviously sensing she was being watched.

"You're wondering why I brought you here."

Lily chuckled. "That would be putting it mildly."

Samantha Browne arranged a scone on a plate and put it down in front of Lily. Lily's mouth watered and her stomach growled, but she forced herself to remember her manners.

"My...my family tells me I have a bleeding heart. My husband claims I can't stand to see anyone or anything suffer." A tiny laugh escaped her perfect mouth. "I guess a better way of putting it is that I'm constantly sticking my nose into things that aren't my business."

She put a cup of coffee down in front of Lily, then gestured toward the delicate pitcher of cream. "But when I see a lovely

11

young woman standing in a vacant lot, drenched to the bone, my imagination gets the best of me. I can't conceive of any scenario that would have put you there. So you see, Miss Sawyer," she added with a smile, "I have to find out. And if I can offer you something to eat and a warm bath while you're here, so much the better."

Lily poured a tiny amount of cream into her coffee, then stirred. "It's Mrs., but please, call me Lily."

Samantha's head jerked up. "You're married?"

"Widowed, actually," Lily responded, picking up the warm cup and wrapping her fingers around it. She could have avoided this entire trip if she'd accepted her employer's assistant, Donald South's, proposal. It would have solved her money problems, instead she solved them herself...which is why she was here, hiding from the world.

Samantha quickly turned away. "Oh, I'm...very sorry. I...I didn't mean to pry."

Lily appreciated the sentiment. "That's all right. It's been two years now. Seems like a lifetime ago."

"So, Lily, why did I find you soaking wet on the outskirts of a little logging town?"

"Well, do you always drive around after a storm rescuing drowned rats?"

Oddly enough, Samantha Browne blushed. "Of course not. Actually," she added as she sat beside Lily on the sofa, "I was coming from my cabin. My—" She stopped abruptly, put her hand to her mouth, then continued. "My parents owned a small cabin in the woods, and after they died, I couldn't find it in my heart to sell it. I drive up there occasionally to make sure it's in order."

Lily gave her a noncommittal smile, then turned to study the fire. "I'm looking for work."

"Oh? What do you do?"

"I've worked as a cook and housekeeper since my husband's death." No need to go into his history. It wasn't important; not to her, not anyone else. "I cooked in a boarding-house in San Francisco. Until it burned down." She didn't bother to mention that after that, she was hired by the man who would attempt to find her and if he did, she would fear for her safety.

Samantha brightened. "You're a cook?"

Lily gave her shoulders a weary, sardonic shrug. "Now, don't tell me you're looking for one."

Samantha sat forward. "Well, not me personally, but the loggers are always wearing out the cooks. Why, that's perfect! You need a job?" Samantha nodded with finality. "You've got one."

Lily's weariness lifted slightly. "Now, if you can find me a room, we're in business."

"Oh, but I can do better than that," Samantha enthused. "How...how would you like your very own little cabin?"

Lily faced her, her mood lifting more. "Your cabin? Are you sure?"

"I'm positive. It's less than a mile from the logging camp. The kitchen is equipped for cooking large quantities. Someone from the camp will come by daily to pick up the food. There's a smaller cabin adjacent as well. Maudie Tupper, the previous camp cook, lives in it. She's not well." Samantha tapped her chest. "Lung trouble. Had to quit cooking when she started coughing up blood—Oh," she said, putting her hand over her mouth. "I hope that doesn't bother you."

Lily felt a wash of sympathy for the sick woman. "Of course not. It'll be nice to have the company. But...why doesn't she live in *your* cabin?"

Samantha's laugh sounded forced. "Oh, she refuses to. But

13

don't worry, her cabin is snug and dry, and she'd love to have another woman around."

Lily couldn't believe her good fortune. She was wise enough not to question it. This was perfect. She didn't care if the whole cabin had fallen into decay, it was hers to use. She'd clean up and make it shine. She'd make a home for herself, something she'd never had in her whole life. She and the late, not-so-great Black Jack Sawyer had lived in nothing but single rooms over saloons and taverns. Her luck was changing, and she knew better than to look a gift horse in the mouth.

Ross dismounted and stretched his aching back. The trip over the mountains into the valley was one he always hated. The valley was hot and dry, even in October. Twin Hearts had the blessed ocean breeze to keep it cool all year long.

He dragged in a breath of crisp air and glanced at the cabin. Thank God, he was home. Smoke chugged from the chimney. He grinned. Samantha's doing, no doubt. Before he left, he'd had an infestation of fleas in the cabin, so he moved his clothes and his bedding to Sam's for fumigation before they treated the place. Yawning, he hoped she'd returned them, but if she hadn't, he'd pick them up later. What he needed now was sleep. If it was on a bare mattress, so be it. He crossed to the lean-to and unsaddled his mount, brushed him down, and fed him.

The vegetable garden caught his eye as he and Red trudged toward the cabin. It was free of weeds. Maybe Maudie had been feeling better. He hoped so. As he stepped onto the porch, he glanced at the sky. Morning fog clung to the tops of the Douglas firs. He'd risen long before dawn to get home, anxious to sprawl out in his own bed and sleep for the rest of the day.

He was about to open the cabin door when Red growled.

Ross paused and opened the door a little, telling Red to stay. The dog continued to growl deep in his throat, but heeded Ross's command.

Suddenly wide awake, Ross stepped into the room and realized he had no weapon but his knife, sheathed to his belt.

The bedroom door was closed. Before he could stop him, Red bolted toward the door, pushing it open with a bang. He raced into the room, barking furiously, then suddenly yelping in pain.

The scene before Ross unfolded in slow motion, as if the powers that be held the reins of time. His dog, still yelping, flung his head from side to side as something gray and feral clung to his muzzle. Ross pulled out his knife, and before he could attack the critter that was attacking his dog, he was hit from behind, rendering him so weak he fell to his knees.

His knife fell to the floor and was swiftly kicked away from him. He shook his head to clear it, suddenly aware that he was not alone in the room. But Red's constant yelping propelled Ross across the room to try to aide his dog.

"Tell your dog to lie down."

The voice came from behind him. "What the hell?"

"Tell your dog to lie down if you want him to stop his howling."

Still a bit dazed, Ross did what was asked, and immediately what ever was attacking the dog released its hold, jumped to the floor and meandered off. He saw the swish of a fluffy tail as it disappeared out the door,

"A goddam cat?" he roared.

Red crawled toward him, and Ross inspected the dog's muzzle. Grateful it wasn't worse, Ross, still on his knees beside his injured pet, turned to look at his assailant.

He looked up and found himself staring into the familiar barrel of his own hunting rifle.

"Who are you?"

A woman? Attempting to focus, he shook his head again and saw a pair of pale, slim calves peeping out from between the edges of a frilly pink dressing gown.

His gaze slid up slowly, over rounded hips and a firm, generous bosom. Her hair, loose and wild around her face, was red as a firestorm, and her green eyes held not an ounce of fear.

"Me?" he roared. "Who the hell are *you*, and what are you doing in my bedroom?"

The woman looked momentarily surprised, then spat, "This is *my* bedroom. Get out before I blow your head off."

With a movement that belied his size, Ross grabbed the gun and leaped to his feet.

"Now," he growled, ignoring the fear that suddenly crept into her eyes. "I'll ask you again. Who in the hell are you?"

She recovered quickly. Moving away only slightly, she volleyed, "Who are *you*?"

This was getting them nowhere. "My name is Ross Benedict, and this is my cabin, therefore, my bedroom."

Her eyes narrowed. "That's a lie. I know who this cabin belongs to, and it surely isn't you. Now what do you really want?"

Stupefied and angry, he continued to stare at her. "I want to know what in the hell you're doing in my bedroom. Is that so hard to understand?"

She returned an angry glare. "This is my bedroom and my cabin, at least for now. And…and stop staring at me, you ogling dolt."

Brows furrowed, Ross turned away, crossing his arms firmly over this chest. Red made a whimpering sound at his feet. "I asked you before, who in the hell are you?"

"Why should I tell you? You're the one who's trespassing."

He spun around, catching her just as she tied the sash of her dressing gown, a movement that pulled the robe tightly over her generous bosom. As a thickness gathered in his groin, a thought wormed into his brain. He uttered a stream of curses that turned the air blue.

"Sam. Samantha put you up to this, didn't she? Damnit all to *hell*!" He released the woman and slammed his fist into the door—and it went right on through.

Behind him, the woman let out a shriek.

He turned on her, ignoring the wood splinters that dug into his flesh. One of her hands covered her mouth. The other clutched the lapels of her gown tightly at her throat.

"She did this, didn't she? Sam put you up to this."

She removed her hand from her mouth long enough to ask, "S…Samantha Browne?"

"Yes," he answered, his voice filled with silky understanding. "Samantha Browne."

The woman swallowed hard. "How…how do you know Samantha Brown?"

Ross was sick of the game. "You know very well how I know her."

The woman's demeanor changed. No longer cowering against the bed, she planted her fists on her hips and studied him. "No, I don't. Why don't you tell me? You come in here acting like a raving lunatic, frightening me half to death. I think I deserve an explanation. That is, if you're capable of stringing that many words together at one time."

Ross was momentarily surprised at her unusual tactics. After all, most women threw themselves at him. And no eligible woman, or any other for that matter, had ever called him an ogling dolt or a raving lunatic. Once, of course, Trudy had called him her raging stallion, but that was after a particularly satisfying night in her bed. It had been a compliment, not

17

flung at him like pig swill. This red-haired witch was different from all the others, he'd give her that.

"She's my sister. As if you didn't know." He turned and studied the hole he'd put in the door. "And this is my cabin. I live here."

She gasped. "Your...your sister?"

Ross's temper was volatile, but after an explosion, he mellowed out quickly. "Now you understand. I don't know what little game Sam is playing, but this is *my* place. If the two of you thought this little ploy would work, well, damnit, think again."

"I don't believe I understand you," she said carefully. "If we thought *what* would work?"

"Ah, hell. Never mind. Just get dressed and get out of here. The little plan backfired, and I'm dead tired." He yawned, purposely emitting a loud, disgusting sound before pulling his shirt from his pants.

She didn't move.

"You gonna send your attack cat after me?" he asked.

They stared at each other, her gaze haughty and cool, his blatantly, purposefully sexual, while he unbuttoned his shirt. He pulled it open and scratched again, giving her a wide view of his naked chest. That usually frightened tight-assed women away.

Suddenly, she shoved him, catching him off balance. He crashed into the wall again.

"Get out of here," she ordered. "I'm renting this place from Samantha Browne, and if you have a problem with that, see her. *I'm not leaving*."

Ross pushed himself away from the wall, feeling the knot of fury twist in his chest. He'd see Sam, all right, and he'd take her over his knee and tan her hide. Then he'd return and toss this flame-haired harridan out of his cabin on her backside.

Picking up his rifle, he stormed from the room. "This isn't over, woman. When I come back, I'd better find you packed and gone, damnit."

~

Lily closed her eyes and sagged to the bed, her heart pounding so hard she worried that it would crack her ribs. She allowed herself a moment to pull herself together, then hurriedly dressed and went into the kitchen to start preparations for the loggers' lunch.

The cat, which she eventually called Ruby, rubbed against her skirts. "Nice job, girl. We're quite a team."

The back door opened, and Maudie came through, tying her apron strings behind her. "What was all that commotion in here a while ago?"

"Some big oaf busted the bedroom door, claiming this was his place."

Maudie chuckled. "Sounds like Ross to break down a door."

Lily turned from the stove. "You know him?"

"Well, yes. It's his cabin, dear."

Puzzled, Lily didn't know what to think. "Why would that young Mrs. Browne rent it to me? Did she really think it would be empty?"

Maudie frowned. "Maybe. Ross is overseer for the mill and does all the buying and selling. Maybe she got confused."

"And her brother actually does own the cabin, then?"

"Well, they own it together, I'd say."

Certain there had to be some reasonable answer for all of this, Lily vowed to find a way to see Samantha Browne at her earliest convenience.

As she worked, she thought of the man who had just left. Man? She forced a dry laugh. More like a bear. She was no small women, but he was many inches taller than she. Shoulders so wide he'd had to turn sideways to get through the bedroom door. But he was a bear, in breadth *and* manners. He merely dressed like a man to cover his crude, beastly behavior.

Remembering his final threat, she stiffened. She was not leaving. She was *not*. She was curious to know, however, why Samantha Browne would rent her a cabin that was already occupied.

Chapter Two

Ross stormed into the house catching Sam by surprise. When he slammed the front door, she visibly jumped. She looked up from the desk to see who had startled her and give him a warm smile.

"How was the trip? I'm glad you're back." She bent over a ledger. "I've got to get the books done before Derek gets home. Did you bring the lumber order from Chico?"

Her calmness set his blood boiling. "Just what in the bloody hell do you think you're doing?"

She looked up again, mildly surprised. "Doing? I told you. I'm getting the b—"

"That's not what I mean and you now, it, Samantha Mae Browne!"

Taking in a deep breath and expelling it slowly, Sam closed the ledger on the desk, then folded her hands in her lap. She managed a smile. "You've...you've been to the cabin."

"I want her *out*!"

"Oh, Ross, I can't do that." Sam's face was pinched with concern. "She had no place to go, and—"

"And you thought you could foist her off on me, is that it?

Oh, no, you don't. I promised myself I'd never let you do this to me again, Sam, and I won't."

She rose from the desk, primly straightened the front of her blue flannel skirt, then stepped in front of him. "I...I don't know what on earth you're talking about. Her...name is Lily Saw—"

"I don't want to know her name, damnit!"

Samantha sighed, then spoke to him slowly. "Her name is Lily Sawyer. She's a cook who...who came to me looking for a job. They need a cook at the camp, Ross, you know that as well as I."

Ross felt like punching a hole in another door, but he still had splinters in his fist from the last one. "What's she doing in my cabin?"

"There was nothing accessible close enough to the camp."

"There still isn't."

Samantha turned away, disgusted. "Oh, quit bellowing. I've promised she can stay there until...until something comes available."

Ross tried to keep a lid on his temper. He didn't trust Sam. He'd discovered years ago that when his forthright sister hesitated in mid-sentence, she was up to no good.

"I don't believe this all came about out of the blue, Sam." He jabbed a finger at her. "No, you cooked this up, thinking that if you plunked some woman down in my cabin, I'd be too much of a gentleman to kick her out. Well," he continued, still bellowing, "you're wrong." He turned to leave.

"I'll never forgive you if you toss her out, Ross."

Stopping mid-stride, he turned, giving her a suspicious glance. "What?"

There was no wicked gleam in her big, innocent brown eyes. "I said, I'll never forgive you—"

"I heard what you said," he interrupted. For all the times

22

she'd tried to marry him off, she'd never threatened him this way before. It was unnerving. Unsettling. So damned unlike her. Suddenly, he heard himself asking, "Where in the hell am *I* supposed to live?"

Shrugging expansively, she answered. "The cabin is big enough for both of you, isn't it?"

The thought staggered him. "Just how in the devil would that look?"

"Oh, for heaven's sake, Ross. We're not talking about Boston drawing room society. This is Twin Hearts, California. Lord, it's on the edge of civilization. One more push and we'd all fall into the Pacific. Anyway, Maudie is there. She's so close, she practically lives in the cabin, anyway."

Ross moved toward the door again. "If this is your way of compromising her, forcing me to marry her because of it—"

"Oh, don't be foolish. I wouldn't do such a thing. And anyway, it…it won't be for long, Ross, truly."

Noting the tell-tale hesitation in her voice again, he flung open the front door and warned, "Damned right, it won't."

He was halfway to the cabin when he turned back. Because of his anger at Sam, he'd forgotten to pick up his clothes.

Lily finished cutting up the apples and tossed them with flour, sugar and cinnamon. She set them aside while she rolled out the pie dough. She'd been amazed at the kitchenware that had been stored in a shed behind the cabin. And the kitchen was separate from the rest of the place. Well, a separate room, anyway. Samantha had told her that when her parents were alive, her mama had cooked for the logging crew, so the kitchen was not only a separate room but a very large one. After scrubbing every square inch of it, Lily had felt at home.

She draped a circle of raw dough over a pie tin and, with gentle fingers, pressed it against the bottom, then repeated the process until she'd covered the bottoms of six tins.

Memories of what had happened earlier continued to erode her self-control, and by the time all six pies were ready to bake, her hands were shaking. She glanced out the window, hoping the madman was gone for good. All morning, she'd been nervous and edgy waiting for the brute to return.

When she'd first heard noises outside, she'd been so frightened she thought her heart would explode. She'd kept the rifle near the bed from the very first night, and her sense of self-preservation had always overcome her fears. But she thought with a weary smile, he'd gotten the rifle away from her with ease. She just thanked the good Lord she'd heard him coming. At least she'd had time to throw on the dressing gown Samantha had loaned her. Otherwise...

She let out a whoosh of air. Otherwise, he'd have caught her without a stitch on. He could have... She shuddered and leaned against the counter, trying to keep her breath even, trying not to think about what he *could* have done.

And she had no idea that making the dog lie down would allow Ruby to release his muzzle and walk away. It was a lucky hunch.

Hearing a noise, she lifted her gaze to the window. Her heart sank. He was back. She slipped three of the pies into the oven, then picked up a knife and began slicing vegetables for the stew she was preparing for the logging crew's lunch the following day.

She would not let him toss her out. She would *not*. If he refused to leave, she would just make the best of a bad situation. At least Maudie was there as a chaperon, although Lily wondered what good the poor woman would be. Maudie hadn't left her own little cabin since the day Lily arrived except to come in and cut vegetables. Lily had spent hours sitting with her watching her nap. She was surprised she'd even heard the ruckus earlier. No, she wasn't much of a chaperon, but no one had to know that.

She felt rather than heard the man behind her. The hairs on the back of her neck bristled.

He cleared his throat.

Attempting to compose herself, she turned, hoping her expression showed none of her inner turmoil. He was as big as she remembered. Bigger, perhaps. And he was a hairy beast. His dark hair was far too long, curling wildly about his ears, and she was certain his full, thick beard hadn't been trimmed in months.

They studied each other warily before he finally spoke.

"I guess I can tolerate having you here for a while. But just so you know, I made the frame for the bed myself, to fit *me*. I'm not giving up my bed for anyone, not even a damned woman. Stay out of that room. I don't want you fussing around, trying to clean it or straighten it. I'll give you time to get your things out of there, but from now on, I don't want to find out that you've set foot in there. Is that understood?"

Lily's blood boiled and she clutched the knife handle hard. "Let me get this straight, Mr....Benedict ?" she began, straining to contain her temper. "You're graciously allowing me to stay in your cabin, is that correct?"

He gave her an abrupt nod.

"But I'm not to expect to sleep in your precious bed or set foot in your bedroom."

Another imperious nod. "The bedroom is mine."

Still trying to restrain herself, she said, "I wouldn't dream of stepping into your domain. I'll have my things out of there as quickly as possible. The bed wasn't all that comfortable, anyway," she lied. The first night she'd slept in it, she'd thought she'd died and gone to heaven. But then, anything was better than what she'd been accustomed to.

He turned to leave. "Good. Then it's settled."

"Not quite."

He stopped at the door. "What do you mean?"

"I have a job to do here. I spend all day cooking for the loggers. I never allow anyone else in my kitchen. Nor do I have time to fix something special for you." She didn't add that she always prepared three meals a day for Maudie.

"I can eat whatever you fix for the crew," he answered almost congenially.

"I don't think so." Her voice was edged with iron.

"Well, sure I can," he answered eagerly.

She pulled in a breath, letting it escape audibly. "No, I don't think you understand." She placed her fists on her hips and stared at him. "The bedroom is yours? Fine. The kitchen is mine, and the same rules apply."

"What?"

She turned back to her vegetables, amazed that she could handle the knife without lopping off a finger. "You heard me, sir. You are not to enter my kitchen unless I invite you. Is that understood?"

He bellowed like a bull moose behind her, then finally retorted, "Ah, what the hell do I care? Your food probably tastes like bird shit anyway."

She allowed herself a small smile. "If you're familiar with the taste of bird droppings, Mr. Benedict, I'm sure you'll have no trouble foraging for your meals outside, like the other animals."

When she was certain he was gone, she expelled a long, shaky breath and leaned against the counter for support. She heard—and felt—the door slam and watched as he stormed to a tree stump, positioned a log on top of it, then proceeded to chop

26

the wood into kindling with the ease of a child breaking up matchsticks.

She shuddered and briefly closed her eyes. Battle lines had been drawn.

$\sim$

An hour later, Ross was still chopping wood. He had enough to last the winter—maybe several winters. He tossed the last of the wood onto the pile, then flung the ax, carefully aiming for the tree stump. The blade hummed from the impact, and the handle quivered.

He was soaking wet. And exhausted. Wiping his forehead with his shirtsleeves, he started for the cabin. The smell of fresh-baked apple pie wafted toward him. His stomach grumbled and he swore. He hadn't a thing to eat since four o'clock in the morning, when he'd begun his ride home chewing on the last of the biscuits he'd gotten in Chico.

Stepping to the cabin door, he shoved it open, letting it slam against the wall. Pie aroma was stronger inside the cabin, and he steeled himself against it, crossing purposefully to the bedroom.

As he walked past the bed, he saw her nightgown and dressing gown still lying across it. He grabbed them in his fist, intent on tossing them out into the living room. Instead, he brought them to his face and inhaled the fresh feminine scent that lingered on the fabric. Warmth transfused his groin, making him hard, and he tossed the garments onto the bed, cursing his weakness.

He grabbed a towel and soap from the washstand and stormed into the living room, crossing quickly to the front door. "Get your damned frilly things out of my bedroom!"

His angry roar nearly caused Lily to drop the pie she was retrieving from the oven. Juggling it carefully between hot pads, she placed it on the counter below the window with the others.

He'd stormed out again, slamming the door. With a wry smile, she wondered if he ever did anything by half measure.

Stepping away from the counter, Lily observed her mess. She would need plenty of hot water to clean up the stack of dishes and pots that cluttered the countertop and the sink.

With the pail in her grip, she went outside and crossed to the pump, praying there would be water. It had been hit and miss since she arrived. Sometimes the water flowed freely, other times she couldn't raise a drop. She primed the pump. Nothing happened. Uttering a mild oath, she picked up the pail and strode purposefully toward the river that ran swiftly by the cabin.

She was just leaving the footpath that ended in the clearing when she saw him. Her heart leaped in her chest, and she quickly turned away, but not before she saw him standing in the knee-deep water bringing a soapy hand to his groin.

Pressing her fingers to her mouth, she stumbled up the path, her heart still hammering. She tried not to think about what she'd seen as she looked for another access to the river, but the vision would not go away.

Never had she seen so much body hair on a man. His chest was thick with it, as was…the place below. She refused to think about what else she'd seen in that place below. This man, with his strategically placed body hair and his immense size, made her wonder if all men were so endowed. Compared to him, Jake had been a boy.

She tried to force another wry smile as she picked her way

through the brush toward the other path, but her mouth trembled instead. Sometimes she missed Jake terribly. Not that he'd been the perfect mate, for he hadn't. But their intimacy—until she learned of his unfaithfulness. She realized, to her consternation, that she still missed the part of her marriage that led to the bedroom.

Spotting the river through the trees, Lily shook thoughts of Jake from her head and moved quickly toward the water. As she bent near the water's edge, her foot slipped on the wet grass and she scudded, rump first, into the river. Her shriek of surprise pierced the quiet air and she struggled to stand, only to find the current so strong she was unable to get her footing.

She looked up just as Ross Benedict came crashing through the trees, wearing nothing but a pair of jeans, buttoned only halfway to his navel. His chest hair was still wet. Hard muscles bunched in his shoulders and arms.

He reached toward her, and because she had no alternative, she allowed him to pull her from the water. His touch was firm and warm and surprisingly electric.

"What in the hell were you trying to do?"

She was becoming accustomed to his bellow. "I was getting water and I slipped," she answered tersely.

He took in her soggy appearance. "What were you doing way over here?" he demanded, glancing at the slippery, muddy ledge she'd tumbled from. "The path is—" He stopped in mid-sentence and studied her.

She picked up the pail and brushed past him, unwilling to look at him lest he see the embarrassing bloom on her cheeks. "I can get water from any part of the river I please. I don't have to get it from…from that path."

He gripped her arm and she turned, surprised.

"Give me the pail." His dark eyes gave off a strange light.

Swallowing convulsively, she handed him the pail, then

trudged toward the cabin, holding her water-soaked skirts above her ankles.

Kicking off her wet slippers at the door, she went straight to his bedroom, picked up her valise and crossed to the kitchen. She huddled near the stove and undressed, relieved that she'd finished cooking for the day.

Tossing furtive glances at the closed door, she changed into dry clothes, praying the bull had enough sense to stay out.

She was buttoning the last of the buttons on her dress when he knocked on the kitchen door. "What is it?" Her voice sounded shrewish. She didn't care.

"I've..." He cleared his throat. "I've...ah...got the water."

She opened the door and took the pail from him, thanking him with an austere nod. She noticed that he still wore no shirt, and she tried to ignore the unwelcome flutter of pleasure low in her belly.

Chapter Three

By late afternoon, Ross was so hungry he felt his stomach gnaw at his backbone. He shrugged into his buckskin jacket, saddled his mount, and rode into Twin Hearts to see Trudy.

The nice thing about Trudy, he thought as she pulled him into her kitchen, was that she didn't expect anything from him. She was there when he needed her, and what he needed now, before anything else, was to be fed, even if Trudy wasn't the best cook in the world. He shoved aside thoughts of savory apple pie and hot stew, thick with chunks of venison and vegetables from his own damned garden.

"Poor darling," Trudy crooned, setting a plate of meat and cabbage in front of him. "You look absolutely worn out."

She sat down across from him and, as she always did, tucked her bare toes under his thighs. It usually readied him for what came later, but tonight it did nothing. Hell, he was probably too hungry to get horny.

Trudy was usually quiet, which he appreciated, but tonight she was full of chatter. As she blathered on, he studied her between bites of bland meat and sour cabbage. He'd always thought her reasonably attractive, but tonight, for some reason, her brassy, frizzy hair looked like it would spark dry tinder and her face appeared blotchy.

He pushed his plate away even though he hadn't finished eating. He was no longer hungry.

"Is that all you're going to eat?" Trudy rose and came to him, touching his forehead with the back of her hand. "Hon, your face is burning up." She ran her hand across his chest, then down over his groin. She gave him a not-so-gentle squeeze, then pulled away, surprised. "You aren't even hard, Ross." She busied herself undoing the buttons of his fly, but he removed her hand.

She gave him a questioning look.

He shoved his chair back and stood. "I'm not in the mood tonight, Trudy."

With nervous fingers, she clutched her dressing gown over her generous bosom and looked at him, her eyes filled with a strange fear. "Did I do something wrong, hon?"

Ross crossed to the fireplace and stoked up the fire. "It's not you, it's me." And he knew it was, although he sure as hell didn't know why.

He turned from the fireplace as she walked toward him, and when she pressed herself against him, he touched her back gently but didn't pull her close. The scent she wore was familiar, but he suddenly found it sweet and cloying and far too strong. Like she'd taken a bath in the stuff.

"You're scaring me, hon. I've never known you to pass on a toss in bed."

He gave her a pat on the rump, then turned away to stare into the fire. Trudy was a fine woman, although Ross knew that he wasn't the only man she saw. For want of a better term, he guessed she was a widowed housewife/whore. Her husband had been dead for two years, killed in a logging accident. She had no other means of support except for what men decided to give her for her services. She not only slept with them, she fed them and nursed them, listened to their complaints and soothed their sorrows. She had a good heart.

But he didn't want to crawl between her thighs. Not tonight, and maybe not ever again. It was the darndest revelation, but he simply couldn't imagine bedding her. "I'd still like to come by and talk once in a while."

"Talk? Just talk?" She sounded upset.

"Let's be honest," he said, his voice gentle. "I'm not the only man you see, Trudy. We both know that."

"Well...well, yes," she answered. "But—oh, Ross!" She flung herself at him. "I...always thought that...that maybe someday, we'd—"

He pushed her away as gently as he dared. Her eyes shimmered with tears, and streaks of mascara tracked her cheeks. "I'm never getting married. What we had was a damned fine time in bed. And you're a good woman, Trudy." He touched her chin, nudging her face up. "Remember that. Don't spoil what we had by pretending there was more."

She sniffed, wiping her tears with the sleeve of her robe, smearing her mascara further. "But you will still come to see me?"

He gave her a warm smile. "I said I would, didn't I? You'll have to feed me now and then." He guessed Trudy's cooking was better than bird shit, although not by much.

She stood on her tiptoes and kissed him. "I'll be right back." Her bounteous, dimpled buttocks shifted beneath her dressing gown as she retreated into her bedroom, and when she returned, she had his scarf in her hand.

"Here," she said, unfolding it and draping it around his neck. "You left this here last time. I've kept it in a drawer with my underthings."

33

It smelled generously of her favorite cologne—the very cologne she wore now. He tried not to make an unpleasant face. Bending to kiss her forehead, he said, "Thanks, Trudy. You're quite a woman."

"And you're a special man, Ross Benedict. But I'll admit I don't understand you."

He lifted his jacket off the coatrack and slipped it on. "That makes two of us." He'd come here tonight fully intending to do what he'd always done: enjoy Trudy's bland food, then have a good, lusty tumble in her bed. Instead, he'd found her cooking completely distasteful, and he honestly couldn't imagine sleeping in her bed ever again.

After checking on Maudie, Lily bathed and dressed for bed, then sat curled in a chair by the fire, planning the loggers' menus for the next week. Samantha had promised that tomorrow she would pick her up and they would shop for supplies.

And Lily thought, one eyebrow arching skeptically, she must ask Samantha why she had rented her a cabin that was quite obviously already occupied. By her brother, no less.

Unable to imagine any sound reason for doing such a thing, Lily shook her head and went back to her list.

She found herself glancing up occasionally, wondering when the bellowing bear would come charging in. She had absolutely no interest in knowing where he was. It wasn't her business, anyway. She had hoped he'd never come back.

But when she heard him ride up, she discovered that her heart was pounding hard, and her palms were sweaty. She inspected her list, feigning an interest she didn't feel when he finally entered the cabin, that poor dog at his heels. The dog trotted over to her and sniffed her knees, and Lily was hard pressed not to give him a good scratch between the ears. His wounds from Ruby weren't really all that bad. "Ruby is out for the night," she said to the dog, and as if he could understand her, he gave her with the most grateful look.

Her quick glance turned to the bull's appearance, and she had to admit she was surprised. In spite of the beard and unruly hair, he looked almost elegant in his snug jeans, white shirt, and tan buckskin jacket. A white scarf hung loosely around his neck.

"Evening." His voice was husky and deep.

She swallowed. "Good evening," she answered. She had almost formed a new opinion of him when she got a whiff of him as he walked past her on his way to the cabinet where she knew he kept his liquor. She wrinkled her nose and frowned. He smelled like a bawdy-house pimp, but why should she care? Where he spent his time was no concern of hers. Actually, it didn't surprise her at all that he had to *buy* affection. How he and that sweet Samantha could be brother and sister still baffled her.

❧

"Can I…er…get you something?"

A small brandy would have been welcome, but she shook her head. "No. No, thank you."

With a glass half-filled with amber liquid in his hand, he took the other chair in the room, which sat opposite hers, and stared at her.

She tried not to squirm under his scrutiny. The whole idea of them sharing this cabin suddenly became at the very best ludicrous and at the worst improper. She had known from the start that Maudie was a chaperon in name only, but that had never really bothered her before. Lily wanted to retire to the kitchen, but something kept her seated.

The silence stretched like a taut wire between them, vibrating with unspoken energy.

He set his glass on a round table next to him, then pulled out a small leather pouch. "Mind if I smoke?"

Shrugging nonchalantly, she answered, "It's your cabin."

"Nice of you to remember that," he muttered as he rolled a cigarette.

She pretended to study her list but occasionally glanced at him through the veil of her lashes. The firelight slanted across his face, casting the distinct plans of his features into bold relief. He had a patrician nose, and even with his beard, she could tell that his cheekbones were high and sharp. No doubt, he wore the beard to cover sallow, sunken cheeks. At least she hoped that was true, even though, for some reason, she knew it was not.

"Writing a letter?"

She jumped, unaware that he'd been watching her too. "What?"

He nodded toward the pad in her lap. "Writing to someone?"

"No. It's...it's a list of what the crew will eat next week."

He cleared his throat, then took a long pull on his drink.

The sickening scent of the whore's cologne still hung in the air, and suddenly Lily was anxious to remind him of the battle lines that had been drawn earlier.

"I can't decide if I should put ham hocks in the beans or just bake a ham and put a big, thick slice on each plate. With mustard sauce, of course.

"Then, on Tuesday," she said with a sigh, "maybe mutton pie or ham pie. Of course, I'll have ham left over from the day before...so I suppose I could make another stew. They seem to

36

enjoy stew, and it's easy to make." She forced a small laugh. "All I have to do is prepare it, and it basically cooks itself all day long, and I *do* love the smell, don't you?"

She affected a gasp and brought her hand to her mouth. "Oh, I'm sorry, Mr. Benedict. I do hope the smell of my cooking doesn't bother you."

He took another swig of whiskey and scowled into the fire.

"Then there's the dessert," she went on, hoping he was wallowing in misery. "They're getting apple pie tomorrow. I suppose I could make mince pies, but I think cake would be a nice change. I've got a recipe for a very good marble cake with rich chocolate frosting, or maybe an orange cake would be better. Oh, but that takes so much butter. I know!" she said with an innocent smile. "I'll make a sponge cake and drizzle sweet cream whipped with sugar over it. And fresh wild blueberries on top. What do you think?"

He downed the rest of his drink and slammed the glass hard onto the table next to him. His scowl deepened, showing his dark brows together over his eyes. "G'night." The word came out of his mouth like a curse. "Red!"

She gasped in alarm. "What did you call me?"

"I was talking to my dog." He rose from the chair and stormed to the bedroom, slamming the door behind him.

With an embarrassed smile, Lily turned out the lamp, banked the fire in the fireplace, and went into the kitchen. After unrolling her bedroll in front of the stove, she removed her robe and slid into her bed on the floor.

She'd been called Red all of her life. How was she to know it was his dog's name?

Sleep eluded her, and she knew why. This arrangement was not tolerable. Surely there must be suitable accommodations elsewhere. If Samantha Browne would not help her look, she would find a place herself. It wasn't that she minded sleeping on the floor. When she'd left San Francisco, she'd slept anywhere, and she could do it again.

She hated to give that roaring bear the satisfaction of thinking he'd driven her out, though. That part rankled. Still, she had to leave because she was beginning to feel something else. Something she hadn't felt since before she'd discovered Jake's infidelity. And Lord help her, she'd been alone with Ross Benedict for just one day. It would only get worse.

Ross lay on his side, staring at the door. Briefly rising onto his elbow, he punched his pillows, only to discover it didn't make him more comfortable at all.

He now knew why he couldn't bed Trudy, but he didn't understand it. Hell, he didn't even *like* this Sawyer woman, so how could it be because of her? He had to be wrong. Yeah, that was it. It couldn't be because of her. He'd been feeling a sense of restlessness with Trudy for months. Probably because he knew she was more serious about their relationship than he was. And he didn't want any entanglements.

Trudy was a good ol' gal. Hell, maybe he'd just had a bad night. The next time he went to see her, he'd take her to bed and make up for tonight. That would make them both happy. Yeah, that's what he'd do.

But as he flopped onto his back and studied the ceiling, he was puzzled that the very idea of it didn't make him horny.

Chapter Four

Borden's Chop House sat just back from a magnificent cliff from which one could watch the ebb and swell of the ocean. After their lunch, Lily and Samantha sipped coffee while they waited for the supplies to be loaded onto the buckboard. The ocean was hypnotic; their conversation had been sparse.

Finally, Lily broached the subject of the cabin. "Samantha, if you knew your brother lived in the cabin, why on earth did you rent it to me?"

Samantha poured a dollop of cream into her coffee and gave it a dainty stir. As she tapped the spoon on the rim of the cup, she sighed. "I must have misunderstood my brother's intentions. I…I truly thought he was going to spend the…the entire months of October and November in the valley on the other side of the mountains."

She took a sip of coffee, her big brown eyes innocent as she stared at Lily.

"I see," Lily responded. "Well, now that we know he isn't, perhaps I should find other accommodations."

Samantha's delicate fingers rested at her throat. "Oh, I don't think there's anything else available, Lily."

"Surely there must be *something*."

Samantha followed the flowered pattern on the oilcloth with her fingernail. "But the kitchen at the cabin is equipped for cooking large meals, and it's so close to the camp."

"But your brother lives in the cabin," Lily answered, trying to sound reasonable.

"You like it there, don't you? Isn't it perfect for cooking for the loggers? There really isn't another place like it except at the —" She stopped and pressed her lips together.

"Except where, Samantha?"

"Oh, you wouldn't like it. Really you wouldn't," she said fervently. "Poor Maudie lived there briefly, before she moved into the other cabin on our property."

"Why don't you let me be the judge of that?"

Raising her hands in a gesture of defeat, Samantha stood and pulled her black velvet cape around her shoulders. "All right, but believe me, you won't like it."

Lily rose, hugging her own much thinner cape tightly to her. She was actually anxious to look at the new lodgings. Surely anything was better than where she lived now.

Lily's heart sank when she saw the room. Although it was on land adjacent to the mess hall where the loggers ate, it was a poor excuse for a building by any stretch of the imagination. Dimly lit by one small window, it exuded the stench of dead mice and musty wood. And it had a dirt floor. Something scurried in a darkened corner, and both women jumped, automatically reaching for the other.

Lily swallowed hard and tried not to breathe through her nose. "You mean, the previous cooks actually *lived* here?"

Samantha covered her nose with a handkerchief. "Since Mama died, they've all been men. Until Maudie, and now you."

Lily lifted her skirt and backed toward the door, anxious to get outside. "But even so…"

Once out in the fresh air, they both inhaled greedily.

"Now you can see why the loggers love you, Lily."

She shuddered. Actually, she really could. "If the former cooks kept the camp kitchen like they kept house, it's a wonder the men didn't die of food poisoning."

Samantha took Lily's arm, and they walked toward the buckboard. "Now you know what I mean. The room is nothing more than a hovel."

With a shake of her head, Lily asked, "Is there nothing else?"

They boarded the wagon, huddling close for warmth against the cold, damp air.

"Nothing anywhere near close enough," Samantha said, her voice strangely cheerful. "As I said before, Mama used to cook for the crew. That's why the cabin is as close as it is."

They rocked and rolled down the rutted road that led from the camp. "Ross said he'd be there to help unload the provisions," Samantha said with a bright smile.

Just the sound of his name sent chaotic spasms through Lily's stomach. She didn't know what she was going to do, but suddenly she was angry. If Ross Benedict was any kind of gentleman at all, he'd move out and leave the place to her.

∾

The last of the supplies were tucked away, and Samantha sat at the kitchen table, sipping a cup of fresh coffee. "I've always loved this room," she murmured, her eyes soft.

"Were you raised here?"

She shook her head. "Ross was, but when I came long, Papa insisted we live in town." She smiled. "But I always came with Mama when she cooked. I loved the smells." She inhaled deeply. "I still do. What are you cooking? It smells delicious."

Lily flushed at the compliment. "I'm cooking some mutton for meat pies. It's probably the onions that smell so good."

Samantha glanced at the corner. "What's that?"

Lily followed her gaze. "Oh, that's my bedroll."

Samantha turned quickly. "Your *what*?"

"My...my bedroll."

Samantha stared at her. "Where do you sleep?"

Lily gestured toward the stove. "Over there. It's always nice and warm."

"On the *floor*?"

Lily shrugged. "Of course," she said simply.

Samantha shook her head, clearly puzzled. "I can't believe Ross would make you sleep on the floor."

Lily had no intention of explaining their current arrangement. "Oh, don't blame him, Samantha. I've all but taken over the rest of the cabin. I couldn't very well take his bed too."

Samantha rose, tying the ribbons of her cape together before pulling the hood over her head. "But Lily...the *floor*? Why don't I have Derek bring out a sofa? There's one in my parlor that we rarely use—"

"Nonsense," Lily argued. "It would be pointless, anyway. I won't be here that long. I'm not going to give up looking for another place, you know."

Samantha sighed and straightened the shawl on her cape. "No, I suppose you're not. But, Lily, Maudie will miss you if you leave." She sounded disappointed, as if she expected Lily would abandon her job.

Lily couldn't stop her smile. "Sounds like emotional blackmail, Samantha. Don't worry, I won't quit on you."

Samantha seemed distracted. "What?"

"I won't quit cooking for the logging crew."

"Oh. Oh that's…that's good. Thank you, Lily. I appreciate that." She made her way to the door, then stopped. "I really had hoped—" She gave Lily a small smile and shrugged her shoulders.

"Yes?"

Shaking her head, she answered, "Never mind. I'm so happy we met. By the way, Derek and I are hosting a party next Friday night. Nothing fancy, just a gathering of some of our neighbors. Won't you please come?"

"How nice," Lily answered with a smile. "Thank you, I'd love to. Is there any way I can help?"

"Oh, heavens, I'm glad you asked. My housekeeper has gone to Sacramento to be with her daughter, who's expecting a baby. I'd appreciate any help you can give me."

Lily's smile widened. "Count on it."

With a distracted nod, Samantha turned away and opened the door. "I just wish—Never mind. I'll see you soon, Lily."

Puzzled, Lily watched her leave, then returned to the kitchen. She was sampling the broth from the stewing meat when Ross cleared his throat behind her.

She turned, the big wooden spoon still in her hand. The sight of him still sent flutters into her belly. She would never become accustomed to his size. But one glance at his face and she knew something was wrong. "What is it?"

"It's Maudie," he answered. "She's coughing up blood. I think I—"

43

"Oh, my God!" Lily flung the spoon on the counter and hurried toward him. He caught her arm.

"I'm going to take her down the coast to Santa Rosa," he offered. "It's the closest thing we have to a hospital, and there's always a doctor available."

Lily's pulse hammered. "But...but isn't there a doctor in Twin Hearts?"

"Usually," he answered, "but he had to go to the mill upriver. There was a bad accident."

She pulled her arm free and grabbed her cape off the hook by the door. "I'm coming with you. You'll need someone to keep her comfortable."

"I doubt I could stop you," he murmured as he followed her out the door.

It was late when they returned, and Lily was exhausted. As Ross helped her from the buggy, he said, "I don't mean this to sound cruel or unfeeling, but under the circumstances, we'd probably better keep Maudie's hospitalization to ourselves."

She understood completely. The two of them, unchaperoned, would cause quite a stir. In fact, Lily had decided she would sleep in Maudie's cabin.

Lily went to the kitchen to finish up the chores she'd left undone while Ross unhitched the buggy and saw to the horse. She was putting away the last of the dishes when he came in.

Ross shifted nervously form one foot to the other. "I...I just thought you should know that I'm moving out."

Her heart lifted, then dropped, and she felt a shiver of foolish disappointment, even though it was the very thing she'd hoped for. "You...you are?" was all she could manage.

He combed his strong fingers through his hair. "I'll be next door, in Maudie's cabin, in case, well, in case you need me for something."

The pulse at her throat pumped hard and she automatically pressed two fingers against it. "I thought perhaps I should stay there."

He shook his head. "It's easier for me. I don't mind."

"Will you be comfortable there?" The words slipped out without thought.

"There's a bed. I'll make do."

Lily repressed a shiver of guilt. He loved his bed, and he was willing to leave it. She hardly knew what to say. He was giving up a great deal of personal comfort for her sake, and quite frankly, it surprised her.

He slanted a glance at the stove, where the mutton and onions simmered, cleared his throat again, then left.

Lily was almost tempted to ask him if he wanted something to eat.

When she was sure Ross was out of the cabin, she stepped into the bedroom. A smile tugged at her mouth, for he'd straightened the bedding and fluffed the pillows.

Crossing to the wardrobe, she pulled it open and found his clothes hanging there. She'd often wondered why none of his clothes had been there when she'd moved in. She'd always meant to find out but never thought of it when someone was around to ask. She shut the doors and turned to study the room. It was big and masculine, like he was. The bed was enormous. How well she recalled sleeping in it those nights before he'd charged in, regaining control.

She'd been too frightened at the time to dwell on the events of that morning, but now that she'd come to know Ross Benedict even a little bit, she realized how potent the situation could have been. If he walked in on her now, wearing only the flimsy borrowed dressing gown, what would happen? Would he pull it away and look at her? Would she let him, or, for that matter, would she encourage him to do so?

Suddenly feeling weak in the knees, she sat down on the edge of the bed and took a deep breath as her heart clubbed her ribs. When she caught her breath, she stood and walked around to the other side of the bed, studying it as she moved. He was a big man. A normal-sized bed would probably make him feel as though he slept in a cradle.

His scarf was wrapped loosely around the bedpost. She picked it off and brought it to her face, drawing in the scent. With a sound of disgust, she hurled it away. It was drenched with the whore's cheap cologne.

Lily marched to the door, flung it open, and stepped through, pulling it shut soundly behind her. She realized that the whore had probably slept in his bed until she showed up, putting a crimp in Ross's wild lifestyle.

A gnawing hurt that she didn't understand gripped her stomach, and she went into the kitchen, busying herself with the crusts for the meat pies.

As she worked on the dough, she worked on her feelings as well. The man was one step up from an animal. He wasn't worth her hurt or her concern, and he certainly wasn't worth worrying about. If she were lucky, he'd spend every night with his whore. At least that way, he wouldn't be around, constantly annoying her. And to think she'd almost offered to feed him! Thank God, something had brought her to senses.

Maybe she could use his bed if she fumigated it first, but it would be just her luck if the whore's smell had already seeped into the bedding and the mattress to the point where she'd never get rid of it. No, she thought, mercilessly pummeling the dough, she wouldn't set foot in that room again. She'd pretend it didn't exist. She hoped mice nested in the mattress, producing offspring for many, many generations.

A little voice in her head tried to ask her why she was so angry with a man she barely knew, a man who had every right to live his own life. She soundly silenced the prying, snooping little voice. Somehow it felt good to feel something again, even if it was a foolish, inexplicable anger.

~

"You've moved out?" Sam sounded genuinely upset.

"I've moved out, Sam. So you see, your plan didn't work."

"Oh, for pity's sake, Ross. You keep blathering about that, and I...I haven't the faintest idea what you're talking about." She folded the newspaper and put it on the kitchen table, presumably so Derek could read it in the morning. "Where are you staying, then?"

He spooned a generous serving of her rice pudding into a bowl, then doused it with cream to hide the fact that she'd burned the milk and rice, leaving it a dull shade of brown. Hell, he was so hungry, he'd even eat his sister's cooking, which was worse than Trudy's.

"For now, I'm sleeping in the shed," he lied, downing the pudding quickly so he wouldn't have to taste it.

She made a sound of disgust. "Oh, Ross. That's an awful little shack."

"Well," he said, "If you have room here—"

"No, I don't, and you know it," she interrupted. She began to pace. "I suppose that shed could be cleaned out and made presentable."

Suddenly she turned on him, her hands on her hips. "Did you know Lily sleeps on the floor?"

47

He'd suspected as much. Where else was there? He didn't even own a sofa. Shifting under her angry gaze, he answered, "Well, she won't have to now. She'll have my damned bed."

"Good!" She spun away and crossed to the window. When she turned, her expression was almost scathing. "How could you let her sleep on the floor, Ross? Mama and Papa taught you better than that."

Ross took a long slurp of coffee to wash away the taste of burned rice. What could he say? How in the hell could he tell her that this Sawyer woman made him do things he'd never thought of doing before. Made him act like an uncouth clod when he really wasn't. With the other women Sam had sent his way, he'd wanted to throttle someone. But Lily Sawyer made him forget his manners and his inherent love of women. Made him roar like a bear and stomp around like a wounded moose. She made him crazy!

"Do you know that she wanted to leave?" At his look of surprise, she nodded. "Yes. Why, she insisted on finding something else, and the only place available close to the camp is that awful, dirty room the other cooks used." She made a face and shuddered. "Fortunately, she found it as loathsome as I did. If you hadn't moved out, I'm afraid she eventually would leave."

"Christ," he muttered. "Now you tell me."

"That's not funny!"

"I didn't mean it to be! Hell, if I'd thought she was going to cave in, I'd have stuck it out."

Samantha unfastened her long, rich brown braid from the back of her head and massaged her scalp. "For heaven's sake. If you act this way in front of her, it's surprising that she hasn't poisoned you."

He laughed in spite of his anger. "No chance of that," he said before he'd even thought about it.

"Oh? How can you be so sure?" Her eyes glittered.

"Because she refuses to feed me," he mumbled as he crossed to the door.

Sam's laughter slapped him in the back like a wet towel. "She *what*?"

"You heard me." He suddenly felt very put upon. His sister should have had more compassion.

"Good for her," she cheered. "I *knew* she had spirit the minute I saw her standing, drenched to the bone, in that empty lot outside of town."

Ross frowned. "I thought you said she came to you looking for work?"

Sam whirled, her dressing gown swirling around her ankles. "I...I said that?"

"Yes, little sister." His voice was dangerously smooth.

She shrugged and skipped away. "What does it matter?"

He shook his head. "I said it before, Sam, and I'll say it again. It won't work."

She gave him a saucy look over her shoulder. "The important thing is that you've treated her terribly. You've been a perfect boor. I don't blame her for refusing to feed you."

Ross noticed Samantha's good table linens stacked on the counter near the door. "Why do you have those out?" His sister might not have inherited their mother's ability to cook, but she was an immaculate housekeeper.

"We're having a party on Friday." She took his empty bowl and put it in the dishpan, sloshing hot water from a teakettle over it.

"A party? And you weren't going to invite me?" He felt disappointed and betrayed.

"Why should I? You've never done anything but make fun of our friends."

"Well, yeah, but...you've always invited me before, Sam."

She lifted her shoulders and sighed. "Oh, come if you want to. I guess I can't stop you."

Her lack of enthusiasm stung him. Sure, he made fun of her friends, but he hadn't meant anything by it, except for the ones she tried to match him up with.

He turned toward the window. The wind had picked up and was blowing the branches of the fir tree against the glass. They scratched and clawed, as if trying to find a way inside. He shivered, thinking about the long, cold ride home. "The weather looks pretty bad, Sam. Mind if I sleep here tonight?"

She picked his hat off the coat tree and threw it at him. "I most certainly do."

At that moment, Derek stepped into the kitchen. "What's going on? I could hear you two shouting at each other from the den."

"Did you know this big boob makes poor Lily sleep on the floor?" Sam's fists were balled at her hips.

Derek backed up a step and put his hands up, as if to fend her off. "This has nothing to do with me."

"Aw, hell, Derek," Ross mumbled. "I didn't know she slept on the floor. I didn't *make* her sleep there."

Derek laughed. "Oh, no, you don't. I can't take your side, Ross."

Ross felt another jolt of self-pity. "You won't defend me? I'm innocent!"

Derek scooped Sam into his arms and nuzzled her hair. "And I'm not ready to sleep on the sofa, my man. I'd be a fool to argue with my beautiful wife."

Samantha gave Ross a superior nod. "See? Now, go. You can't sleep here."

He was stunned. "Why?"

She took his jacket off the tree and threw that at him too. "You don't deserve a warm place to sleep tonight," she insisted, shoving him toward the door. "Go to sleep with your horse. It's where you belong." She stroked Red's neck then frowned, gently touching his scars. "What did he get into?"

Ross told her of their first encounter with the cat.

Sam bit back a smile. "Poor Red. He used to like cats."

Ross called his dog and stepped out into the night, cringing as the door slammed against his back. Hell, and damnation. Women. He'd never figure them out.

Chapter Five

Ross hitched his mount in the lean-to, rubbed him down and fed him, then trudged toward Maudie's tiny cabin. He was stiff from the cold, for although the wind had been at his back all the way home, it had gone straight through him. As he passed the kitchen window, he noticed the flicker of a lamp. He looked inside, then pulled away, feeling an intrusive wash of guilt, and surprise.

Lily was in there, sitting cross-legged on top of her bedroll in front of the stove, brushing her vibrant hair. Why wasn't she in his bed, tucked snugly under his covers? What in the hell good did it do for him to sleep in the shed if she was going to insist on sleeping on the damned floor?

With a growling curse, he went inside and shoved open the kitchen door. She gasped in surprise, but when she saw him, she glanced away.

"You might try knocking," she scolded, continuing to pull the brush through her hair.

The lamp gave off enough light to make her hair look like fire. That he experienced a sudden urge to discover if the triangle between her legs was darker or lighter shocked him.

That the thought could wangle space inside his head infuriated him. "What in the hell are you doing in here?"

She slipped her bare feet into her bedroll and pulled it to her waist, then rested on an elbow and stared at him. Her breasts swayed seductively against her nightgown, one resting on her arm. Although he could see only the plumpness against the fabric, his mouth went dry.

"I think it's obvious, Mr. Benedict. I'm retiring for the night."

"Why aren't you in my bed, damn it?" He realized as he spoke that the question held a double meaning for him, and that made him even angrier. The thought had come straight out of nowhere.

She held his gaze and he almost flinched at the glittering fury he saw there.

"I prefer sleeping on the floor," was all she said, although he had a feeling she wanted to say more.

"That's plain stupid," he groused.

"I am not stupid."

"Well, you sure do stupid things," he informed her.

She sat up and put her fists on her hips, a movement that pushed her breasts forward against her nightgown. "Such as?"

His mouth continued to feel like cotton, and he tried not to look at the nipples that pouted against the cloth.

"Such as this," he answered, waving his arm around the room. "And...and such as trying to get water from any spot at the river other than the one I've cleared. Hell, you could have been swept downstream yesterday."

"I had no choice."

He should have left it at that, but he didn't. "Why?"

She turned away, but not before he saw her cheeks blossoming with color. "You know very well why."

He had suspected that she might have seen him bathing, and

the thought aroused him. "Did you like what you saw?" He enjoyed seeing her squirm.

Her gaze met his and she was quiet for a moment before she answered. "I've seen better specimens at the zoo."

He roared with laughter, then turned to go. "Hell, if you're not going to use my bed, I am."

"No, you're not." Her voice was deadly behind him.

Glancing back at her, he asked, "So, what are you going to do about it? Toss me out?"

"Oh, no," she answered, her smile as cold as a witch's heart. "I'll set a match to it while you're asleep."

He considered what she'd said, studying that icy smile, sensing the strength and stubbornness behind it. "You would too."

"Count on it, Mr. Benedict. Now, get out of my kitchen. And next time, knock before you enter."

"Hell," he mumbled as he shoved open the door, "you'd think you were royalty rather than just a damned cook."

Lily let out a whoosh of air and cautiously positioned herself on her back. No gentleman would taunt her like that. A gentleman would not have brought up the subject of his bath at all, even if he'd actually caught her watching. But she knew that Ross Benedict was not gentle, and he only bordered on being a man.

She shuddered as the memory of his nudity grew before her. Oh, he was a man, all right. And, remembering how his soapy hand had held his manhood, she sensed he was quite a man.

Quite a man with the whores. Yes, she thought, suddenly grateful for the little voice in her head. No doubt he was quite a man with his whores. They praised anyone as long as they were paid. Although Lily had only slept with one man in her life, she'd heard enough talk and innuendo to know that size had nothing to do with performance.

She heard the front door slam, then his footsteps as he walked toward Maudie's cabin. Did she feel guilty about not letting him use his own bed?

As she snuggled deep into her bedroll, only slightly uncomfortable as her hipbone dug into the floor, she decided she didn't.

～

Early the following morning, Lily hauled the tub outside, then stripped his bed and shoved the sheets into boiling water heavily laced with lye soap. She added some saltpeter for bleaching, then tossed in his whore-scented scarf, touching it only with the tips of her fingers. While the sheets boiled, she carried out the bedding and hung it on the line that was strung between two oak trees in the yard. Grabbing the paddle she used for the wash, she beat the bedding, sending dust into the air. It was quickly absorbed by the morning fog.

She had no intention of sleeping on the clean sheets, but she couldn't abide the fact that they had the stink of a whore's cologne. Any woman would feel the same way and it had nothing to do with *him*.

"What are you trying to kill?"

Startled, she stopped attacking the quilts, her heart pounding both from exertion and from his sudden appearance behind her.

"The smell of your whore," she snapped without thinking. She cursed her tongue and refused to turn toward him.

"My what?" He sounded amused.

Trying to cover her blunder, she asked, "When was the last time the bedding was washed?"

"What the hell difference does it make if no one's going to sleep in it?"

"There was a smell to it that saturated every corner of the cabin," she answered sharply. "And...and that white scarf of yours too. Or," she added, turning slightly toward him, "does it belong to your whore?"

He gave her a lazy, irritating grin. "Oh, it's mine, all right. Kept warm for me between my sweet whore's thighs."

Heat raced to her cheeks. "Men. You're really such a despicable lot. There isn't a faithful one among you."

Taking the paddle from her, he asked, "Who have I got to be faithful to? I've got no wife. And even if I did, I doubt she'd satisfy me enough to keep me from straying. It's normal for me, you know."

She fumed, remembering those words. He was Jake Sawyer all over again. She watched him beat the bedding and wished she had the paddle, for make no mistake about it, she'd use it on him, and gladly too.

He handed her the paddle, then nodded toward the washtub. "When you're ready to hang those, give me a holler. I'll be in the house, repairing the hole you made me put through the door."

She gasped. "The hole *I* made you—"

"If it weren't for you, it wouldn't have happened." He gave her a teasing smile, then sauntered into the cabin.

She watched him walk away, itching to go after him and smack him in the head. But truly, she was grateful to him. Every time she weakened and thought of how he affected her, he would say something stupid, which would harden her heart against him once again. Thank the good Lord for that. She didn't need to be interested in another man who, like Jake Sawyer, had the morals of an alley cat.

56

~

Ross forced a chuckle, assuming he'd feel a sense of well-being as he walked away. He didn't, even though everything he'd told her about the fidelity nonsense was the truth. Or at least it used to be. Damnit, anyway! What had she done to him?

Maybe she was jealous. He smiled, feeling warm and fuzzy inside. For some strange, inexplicable reason, the thought delighted him beyond words. He had to test the notion further, though.

He thought of Sam and Derek's party, and gleefully rubbed his hands together. He wondered if Trudy was busy that night. The twinge of guilt that wormed into his conscience at the idea of using her was effectively squashed when he decided that the end always justified the means.

~

For Samantha's party, Lily wore the finest dress she owned, a threadbare green faille that set off her red hair and her eyes. She would be sorry when it was too worn-out to wear. She'd long since abandoned the cumbersome steel crinolette frame, taking comfort in the knowledge that the other women in this logging town had forsaken that too.

She stood near the kitchen, watching the other guests arrive. Most were men who owned businesses in Twin Hearts, all accompanied by pleasant, sometimes pretty wives.

Lily had never cared much for parties and was grateful she'd agreed to attend Samantha's only if she could help in the kitchen. She had noted Samantha's visible sigh of relief and wondered why—until she'd tasted Samantha's cooking when she'd stopped by for lunch the day before the party.

As Lily replenished the spiced ale she'd heated for the men, the room, which had been filled with chatter and laughter, suddenly went silent. Two women standing near to her gasped and whispered. Lily looked toward the door to see what the fuss was about, and her stomach did that telltale little dipping dance it always did when Ross Benedict came into view.

He stepped aside, looking huge and handsome—with a woman clinging to his arm.

Lily's heart raced and her stomach hurt. She felt clammy, cold and hot all at the same time. She hated the feeling. Refusing even to look at the woman, she went back to her task and noticed that the container of warm ale she held actually shook in her hands. She retreated quickly to the kitchen.

She was attempting to still her racing heart when the kitchen door swung open and slammed against the wall.

"Oh! I could *kill* him!"

Lily's brief glance at Samantha took in her fury. "Who?" she asked, feigning only a slight interest.

"My brother, of course," was the terse answer.

"Why?" Yes, she really did want to know. She'd only know him a week and she'd already wanted to kill him herself.

Because he brought *her*."

Lily sliced through a loaf of cinnamon bread. "Who is she?" her heart continued to pound.

"She's the town whore, that's who she is. We've always been very proud of the fact that Twin Hearts doesn't have a legitimate whorehouse." Samantha clucked in disgust. "We don't need one. We have Gertrude Harding. And to make it worse, many of the married men in that room have actually... used her services. Can you imagine how uncomfortable they must feel?"

$\sim$

58

"That's really their problem, isn't it? If they didn't choose to stray, they would have nothing to worry about."

"Oh, don't sound so logical, Lily. Everyone knows most men stray on occasion."

"Straying even once is one time too many," she answered. "But as for your brother, perhaps he actually likes the woman."

"Oh, no, he doesn't. He's doing this to get back at me for all of the times I tried to pair him up in the past."

She poured hot water over dirty dishes in the dishpan. "Every New Year's Eve, I'd get him together with one of the respectable single women in the area. *Every year*, I did this, Lily. And do you think he ever thanked me? Do you? Lord, no. He acted like I had a noose around his neck and was leading him to a lynching tree. But this…this takes the cake. He's never flaunted Trudy Harding in my face before. Never."

"Maybe he's trying to tell you something."

Samantha retrieved a large round tray from the cupboard and began arranging cookies on it. "Like what?"

"Maybe he's trying to tell you to stay out of his life."

"Oh, but I *can't*, don't you see? He's his own worst enemy. He *needs* me to…to get his life in order. That's why I—" She tossed Lily a guilt-ridden glance, then cleared her throat. "Oh, bother. I give up. If he wants to…to waste his life whoring around, then, I hope he burns in hell."

Lily couldn't stop her smile. "No, you don't."

"No," Samantha answered on a sigh. "I really don't. But, Lily, I'd so hoped—" She looked at her, longing stamped on her face.

"You'd hoped what?"

Samantha shrugged. "That you…that he…that you and he… Well, you know."

Lily was struck by an illuminating understanding. "Don't

59

tell me you rented me the cabin know full well that your brother would be back."

Samantha was quiet for a moment, then answered, "I'll admit that I did. I really thought... I mean, you'd be perfect together." She fussed with the cookies, arranging and rearranging them on the plate. "How was I to know you'd end up hating each other?"

Lily felt herself redden. She didn't know what she felt for Ross Benedict, but she was beginning to realize that it wasn't hate. "Oh, I wouldn't say we *hate* each other, Samantha."

"But you refuse to cook for him, and that has to be because he's treated you like...like rubbish, which I don't understand at all, because he wasn't raised that way. Truly, Lily. Mama would turn over in her grave if she knew the way he's been behaving."

Lily chose not to talk about her relationship with Ross Benedict. Actually, it would have been impossible to do so. How could she explain something to Samantha that she didn't understand herself?

Hearing furniture scraping across the floor, she turned toward the door just as Derek Browne pushed it open. He smiled and held out his arms to his wife.

"We always have the first dance, sweetheart."

Lily felt another ache in her chest, for the look Derek gave Samantha was filled with love and adoration. She would bet her last dollar that this man had never cheated on his wife.

"Oh, Derek," Sam scolded softly. "I should finish this tray of cookies—"

"Nonsense, Sam," Lily interrupted. "Go dance with the man. I'll finish up." Lily was grateful to be busy in the kitchen, but when the tray was ready, she took it into the other room. It gave her an excuse to get a good look at Trudy Harding.

She and Ross were off in a corner, being completely ignored by everyone else in the room. Still clinging to Ross's arm,

Trudy had the forced look of one trying valiantly to have a good time but failing miserably. But she was pretty. Perhaps a little plump, but she had a very pretty face. As she gazed up at Ross, her big brown eyes looked very much like a smitten puppy dog's. The knot of hurt twisted in Lily's stomach.

But she knew she couldn't dislike the woman if for no other reason than that every other woman in the room did. Ross bent his head to listen as Trudy whispered to him, and panic attacked Lily's insides when she saw him nod, then began walking toward her. She wanted to escape into the kitchen but knew they'd just follow her there.

As they approached, Lily could smell the telltale cologne, and a war waged inside her. She was a fool to let the smell of some cheap scent bother her, but on a purely female level, it rankled.

They stood in front of her, so close she almost choked. It took her a moment to realize it wasn't the smell of the cologne that made her nauseous but the battle going on inside her because of it.

"Miss Sawyer? I'm Trudy Harding." She smiled and extended her hand.

Briefly Lily caught the look on Ross's face, one that dared her to be civil to his date when no one else would. He needn't have bothered. No matter what the woman did or was, Lily discovered she couldn't dislike her. She felt too sorry for her.

Lily took the hand, as calloused as her own, and answered, "It's Mrs., but please, call me Lily."

"Oh, then, you *are* a widow too?" Hope sprang into her eyes.

"Yes. Yes, I am."

"You hear that, Ross?" She playfully swatted Ross on the arm. "I told you that's what I'd heard. Knowing that, I'm sure we can be friends."

61

Lily heard the expectation in her voice. She also sensed the loneliness and the quiet hysteria, for she'd felt them in herself often enough. Every other woman in the room could have sympathized if she'd had a mind to, but none of them would. Widowhood left a woman completely unprepared for the world. In some ways, Lily had been lucky. Jake's unfaithfulness had softened the blow of being alone when he died, for she'd shut him out months before. And her isolation had made her independent. Even before Jake's death, she'd been determined to find a respectable job. Obviously, perhaps through no fault of her own, Trudy Hardin had not.

"I'm sure we could," she heard herself say. "Why don't you stop by and visit sometime?"

Trudy's puppy dog eyes widened. "Oh, you...you wouldn't mind?"

"Not at all." Lily discovered she meant it. In fact, she was looking forward to it—for a whole passel of reasons, not the least of which was to get a better understanding of the cad who would drag this poor soul to a party and subject her to such a miserable time.

Lively strains of "Oh, Dem Golden Slippers" announced the beginning of the dancing. Lily glanced at the fiddler, wanting to escape into the kitchen but not wanting to appear rude.

"Come on, Trudy, let's show 'em how it's done."

"Ross Benedict, you know I can't dance tonight." She looked at Lily and shrugged. "I twisted my ankle earlier this afternoon. That's why I'm hanging onto Ross's arm." She brightened. "Why don't you and Lily dance?"

Lily and Ross both voiced excuses, their words spilling out, jumbling together.

"Nonsense. I know how you love to dance, Ross."

Lily knew she was blushing, for her cheeks were hot.

"Well, it's a lively tune," he answered, his gaze lingering on Lily's face. "I suppose I could."

"Oh, no, I—"

"Ask her nicely, Ross." Trudy punched his arm. "What's the matter with you?"

He mouthed a curse, which Lily read clearly. "That's all right, Trudy. I should get back to the kitchen." She turned to leave but felt a hand on her arm. Instinctively she knew it wasn't Trudy's, for shivers played over her skin.

"May I have this dance?"

Had his eyes held even the slightest bit of derision she'd have told him to take a flying leap off a cliff. But they didn't.

Pulling in a shaky breath, she told herself she could do this as long as the music was snappy and bris. Unfortunately, the moment she stepped into his arms, "Oh, Dem Golden Slippers" became "I'll Take You Home again, Kathleen," and Lily was forced to move slowly around the living room floor, cradled in Ross Benedict's very capable arms.

She wanted to speak, to diffuse the tension she felt at being so close to him, but she was suddenly tongue-tied. Whatever else she thought of him, she couldn't deny that he was a wonderful dancer. He led her over the floor, and she followed him as though they'd done this together a hundred times before.

With a subtle movement, he pulled her closer. She tensed in his arms, but she didn't draw away.

"We fit," he said against her ear.

His chest was hard and wide, and she forced herself to think of something else. It wasn't possible, for she'd seen it naked, and if she lived to be ninety, she'd never forget it. The vision swam before her eyes even yet. "Don't be foolish," she managed to say.

He chuckled, a deep warm sound that teased her flesh. "Always contrary, aren't you, Lily?"

It was the first time he'd said her name. Her skin continued to tingle, and she felt a breathlessness she hadn't felt since she'd been courted by Jake. She had to force herself to stay aloof, to keep her distance, if not physically, then mentally. Equal measures of relief and disappointment sifted through her when the music finally stopped.

She attempted to step away, but he held her fast. Her gaze shot to his, and she saw the hunger in his eyes, fearing he could see the same in hers. "The music has ended."

"I think our music has just begun, Lily." There wasn't a hint of amusement in his dark, dangerous gaze.

She swallowed hard. "You're being foolish again."

His hand was low on her back, and he pressed her against him. She felt the hard ridge of him, even through the thickness of their clothes. Their gazes met again. His held a hint of laughter. "After the intimacies we've already shared, Lily, my sweet, I believe you should call me Ross."

That he would boldly mention their mutual hunger fed her anger. "I think I should call you a cad, Mr. Benedict. Have you forgotten that you brought a companion? How can you leave her at the mercy of these women?"

His gaze didn't leave her. "Trudy can hold her own against anyone. And we're just friends."

She snorted, rather indelicately. "Is that why your bedding is riddled with the scent of her cologne?"

He smiled, crinkly little lines fanning out at the edges of his eyes. "Why, Lily, I do believe you're jealous."

She gasped and pulled away, stunned by such a bold—and ridiculous—remark. "What surprises me, Mr. Benedict, is that your swelled head doesn't throw you off balance and send you toppling to the floor."

With a purposeful stride, she went into the kitchen. Once

there, she sagged into a chair and listened to the thumping of her heart.

She stayed in the kitchen, busying herself with the chore of cleaning up. She wouldn't have set foot in the other room again if the back door was on fire.

Chapter Six

Samantha insisted that Ross take Lily home. Trudy kept up a constant prattle all the way. Lily didn't know whether she was nervous at having Lily with them or whether her chattiness was normal. In either case, it made Lily uncomfortable even though she knew the arrangement made sense. The only other alternative had been for her to stay at Samantha's, but Lily had to set the sponge for her bread before she went to bed, then rise early in the morning to form it into loaves and bake it for the logging crew's lunch.

Much to her surprise, Ross dropped Trudy off first. To Lily's chagrin. Trudy threw her arms around Ross and kissed him. For some reason, the moment her lips touched him, he turned, giving her his cheek.

Lily almost sneered. If he had done that for her benefit, he needn't have bothered. For all she knew, he'd sneak back to Trudy's after he thought she was asleep.

They rode home, the sounds of the team's hooves on the hard-packed earth and the jingle of the bells on the harness the only noise in the quiet air. Red trotted beside the horses, keeping pace like he'd been doing it for years.

As they rolled into the yard in front of the cabin, Lily quickly left the buggy and hurried inside. She was met by an indignant Ruby, who raced out into the night like she had a hot date.

Lily had work to do; she couldn't concern herself with Ross Benedict, although she'd thought of little else all the way home. She should never have let herself dance with him. It was bad enough that she'd felt the stirrings of desire, but knowing that he'd felt them, too, made things worse. She'd been tempted to ask him why he'd supposedly embarrassed Trudy by bringing her to a party where she was so obviously not welcome, but it would have meant starting up a conversation, and she'd thought better of it.

She'd just finished preparing the yeast sponge when she heard the spatter of raindrops against the kitchen window. By the time she'd undressed and crawled into her bedroll, the rain had become a deluge. Huddled in the darkness, she listened to the storm. The wind howled, sending great troughs of rain against the windows.

Behind her, where she'd stored flour and sugar, she heard a menacing drip-drip-drip. Struggling out of her bedroll she lit the lamp and crept to the corner, cringing when she saw the water dribbling down the sides of the containers. She put the lamp down and dragged the heavy staples across the floor, shoving them under the table to keep them dry.

She hadn't been back in her bedroll for more than a few minutes when she felt the first drop of water hit her square in the face. Sliding from the covers again, she relit the lamp and took a turn around the kitchen, discovering many places where water was splattering onto the floor.

She stored everything in danger of getting wet under the table with the flour and sugar, then set a number of pots out to catch the water as it leaked through the roof.

Attempting to get comfortable again, she found that her bedroll was wet, and her pillow soaked through. The smell of the wet feathers made her gag.

It went against every grain of sense she had, but the big, clean bed in the bedroom beckoned. She might be stubborn, but she wasn't stupid. It made no sense to sleep in a rain-soaked bedroll when there was an empty bed only a few dozen feet away. Leaving the kitchen, she crossed her fingers, hoping the roof over the bedroom didn't leak.

Stepping inside, she closed the door and listened. She heard no telltale dripping sounds, and although the room was cold, it felt dry. After draping the extra quilt over the bed, she quickly slipped between the flannel sheets and curled into a ball. A drowsy lethargy spread through her, and she fell asleep.

Maudie's cabin leaked like a strainer. Ross cursed, finally so wet he couldn't even pretend to sleep. Hell and damnation, if she wasn't going to use his bed, *he* was. It made no sense at all for him to catch his death when there was a perfectly good bed going unused.

Dashing to the cabin through the deluge, he and Red stepped inside, and he shut the door against the intrusive wind. He went directly to the fireplace to stoke up the fire. Red curled up on a rug near it. Ross sat close to the warmth until it seeped into his bones, then rose and strode toward the bedroom.

It was dark, but he didn't have to light a lamp; he knew his room by heart. He stripped out of his wet clothes, cursing again when he discovered that even his woolen drawers were wet. He unbuttoned them and slid them down his legs, kicking them off, not giving a damn where they landed.

Shivering, he lifted the edge of the bedding and quickly

crawled into the bed, releasing a luxurious sigh as the soft sheets molded around him.

He reached for his extra pillow—and discovered masses of soft, curly hair instead. "What the—?"

Lily had been dreaming, or she thought she had. His voice convinced her she was not. Coming fully awake, she scuddled up from the bed before she rolled toward him, her heart bounding into her throat.

"Oh, God, oh, God, oh God," she murmured hurrying toward the door.

He got to the door before she did. "No." His voice rumbled out from deep within his chest.

Swallowing hard, Lily clutched at the neck of her flannel gown. "Get out of my way."

"No," he repeated. "I'll be damned if I know what's going on between us, but there's something there. There has been from the beginning, and we both know it."

The room was cold; she began to shiver. "I don't know what you're talking about," she answered, trying to not let her teeth chatter.

"No?" He groped for her hand and pulled it away from her throat. "Here," he said, his voice barely above a whisper. "Touch me, then tell me I'm wrong."

Her hand splayed across his chest, the crinkly hair teasing her sensitive palm. She tried to pull away, but he held her fast. Unwitting desire pulsed through her, and her knees felt weak. He moved her hand over the hard muscles that lay beneath his chest hair, and when she no longer argued, he took her other hand and drew them both lower, over his navel, then lower still.

She heard his labored breathing and realized she could barely breathe herself. When he brought her fingers against his thick, hard root, she felt her knees give way, and the place between her thighs, the place that had been dormant since she'd discovered Jake's whoring three years before, came alive like a sleeping lioness, ravenous with a terrible hunger.

Catching her to him, Ross lifted her into his arms and carried her to the bed. Once under the covers, they clung together, pressing tightly. Lily needed to be closer still, and when he moved his hand up her thigh, taking her gown with it, she encouraged him, lifting up off the bed, helping him remove the cumbersome object.

Mindless with desire, she reveled in the feel of his body against hers, rubbing her nipples against the hair on his chest, throwing one leg over his to bring him closer still.

His hand moved between them, down to her aching delta, and he touched her there but briefly, sending her to a teeth-jarring climax. She lay against him, stunned at what had just happened. There had been release, but at what cost? She felt like a whore. Turning her face away, she felt tears run across the bridge of her nose, down her cheek, and into her hair. Ross pressed her shoulders to the bedding and began kissing and fondling her breasts. Arousal threatened again, and she caught her lower lip between her teeth to keep from crying aloud. She hated herself for needing him, despised herself for wanting him.

He was rigid and large against her thigh, but she fought the urge to touch him. A deep, private part of her still felt shame for the way her body had reacted.

"Ah, Lily, Lily," he murmured between kisses. "Your passion robs me of breath." He moved to her mouth, and she opened for him, taking his kiss, returning it with growing excitement that blotted out logical thought. His beard was soft. She'd never kissed a man with a beard before. She wasn't sure she liked it, but she did like the feel of his lips on hers, his tongue twining with hers. Her arousal grew and she touched his arms, his chest, his stomach, allowing herself to stroke his thick root, moving the skin back and forth until he shuddered and shook beside her.

"Enough!" He pulled her hand away, brought it to his mouth and kissed it. "Do you want me to spend like a boy?"

"No," she whispered, coaxing him to her, spreading her legs to invite him in. He entered her, and the feeling was so exquisite Lily thought she would faint. "Oh," she said, close to tears. "It's been so long...so long."

She put her legs around his back and drew him in as far as she was able while he rocked against her, his breath shaky and harsh in her ear.

She felt it begin again, that helpless sensation of pleasure, and she clung to him, reaching for the magic feeling. It spread through her like honey heated in the sun.

He stiffened, then rolled to his side, bringing her with him. She lay there, too spent to speak, or perhaps too uncertain to do so. She should leave, but there was no place to go that wasn't wet and cold and it was so warm in the bed. He was so warm...

He curled around her, spoon style, and she drifted into sleep again, wishing she didn't have to face him in the morning.

Ross wanted desperately to sleep. He couldn't. How in the hell could a man sleep with a body like Lily's pressed against his chest?

Her breathing was even and deep. Certain she was asleep, he gently fondled her breasts, closing his eyes against the pleasure he didn't know how to feel. His emotions disturbed him. He thought he would crow like a rooster at how she'd responded to it. Instead, he was left shaken by the depth of her passion. And his own.

His hand wandered down over her soft, warm stomach to just above the soft thatch that covered her. He had no self-restraint, for one finger dipped lower through the curls to the cleft beneath, then to the slick, wet flesh of her womanhood. Finding the swelling nub, he stroked her.

She made a sound in her throat, then gasped aloud, a telling sound that proved she had awakened. Curling her leg back over his, she gave him access. It wasn't long before she turned to face him and they came together again, their passions stirring like heady wine boiling over a fire.

Ross resisted the urge to stay inside her, although he wanted to fall asleep that way. He rolled to his back again, and when she turned to face the other direction, he felt a ridiculous foreign sense of loss.

Lily awakened before dawn. Although she felt warm and supremely satisfied physically, dread and regret loomed inside her like an impending storm. Before her feelings for Ross could surface again, she inched away from his big, hard body and slid from the bed.

As she slipped from the room, she realized what had happened the night before had happened because she'd allowed it to. She'd had no choice. Her need had been building for years, but now it was over. She felt in control. She could keep him at arm's length.

When she thought about what they'd done, a breathlessness stole over her that left her hungry for him again. Oh damn. Men were such a faithless lot. Both her father and her late husband had been philanderers. She'd buried her feelings towards them a long time ago, but now there was Ross Benedict, bringing one woman to the party and sleeping with another. Though Lily guessed that probably made her no better than him, she resolved never to let herself be coaxed into Ross's bed again.

She fed the fire in the fireplace, then dressed, hoping the

mountain of work she had to do would keep her from thinking of how wantonly she'd acted the night before. She could not understand how she had experienced an orgasm at the mere touch of his fingers. It had to have happened because she'd been in such need after so many years of abstinence.

Shaking away her thoughts, she entered the kitchen, and her heart plummeted. The pots she'd put out to catch the rain the night before were full, a few brimming over onto the floor. After emptying some of them into two large tea kettles, she poured the rest into larger pots to use later. She had to get the bread started before she mopped and scrubbed the floor. But first she made a pot of coffee.

Just as she finished forming the bread into loaves, Ross knocked on the open kitchen door. "Permission to enter?"

The battle lines they'd drawn on that first day seemed childish now. "Of course." She turned and longing swept through her at the sight of him. Although he was dressed, she could imagine the body beneath the clothing, and she flushed. And his eyes... She'd never noticed how dark they were, like black coffee, and just as hot as they swept over her. There was, however, a hint of anger, or something like it, in his gaze. He went to the back door and let Red out, and Ruby raced inside, disappearing from view. "So, that cat stays out all night?" he asked.

"If she wants to."

"Aren't you afraid she'll get pregnant?"

"She might. How does Red feel about kittens?"

"Actually, he's usually good with cats...until now."

Lily nodded and smiled. "I hope he wasn't permanently traumatized."

The thought that Ruby could be pregnant planted a tiny seed in Lily's brain. What about her? Would she, after one night of intimacy, share the same fate?

No. She had never become pregnant with Jake, and although at first she was sad it hadn't happened, when his true colors were revealed, she was glad.

~

"I've...I've made coffee. Please, help yourself. And...there are some biscuits left over from yesterday in that tin at the back of the stove. There's butter and jam in the cupboard."

He nodded but said nothing as he helped himself. He bit into a warm biscuit than glanced at the ceiling. "I guess I have my work cut out for me today."

"It appears to have stopped raining, at least for now." Their inane small talk grated on Lily's nerves. Needing something to do, she took some of the hot water from the reservoir attached to the stove and poured it into a scrub pail, then added shavings of hard soap. After it had dissolved, she filled the pail with rainwater.

She tried to keep her mind on her scrubbing, but just knowing he was watching her made her stiff and self-conscious. She sensed that his thoughts were the same as hers, but she knew she couldn't talk about what had happened the night before. What could she say? That it shouldn't have happened? That it should never happen again? She knew all that. She hoped he did, too.

"Listen," he began. "About last night—"

"It should never have happened," she interrupted breathlessly.

Ross studied her as she dropped the brush into the pail and rested on her knees. For some reason he couldn't understand, he hated to see her this way, washing his floor like some dreary scrub woman.

"No, I suppose you're right. It shouldn't have happened. But I—"

"It won't happen again. I...I have no excuse for my bold behavior. I'm sorry," she said contritely. "I don't know what came over me. Please, please, just forget it happened."

"Forget it happened? How in the hell am I supposed to do that?" He was angry now, Angry at the words that told him so clearly how she felt. He stood, then walked around to face her.

Her head was bowed. "Please," she pleaded. "Don't make me feel any worse than I already do."

His anger turned to hurt. He hadn't been able to understand his feelings either, but beneath it all, he felt damned good. Never had he been so sure that something was right, and here she was, telling him flat out that it had been wrong.

She raised her hands to her hair and fussed with it, a motion that brought his gaze to her breasts all snug and pressed tightly against her gown. The memory of how they felt in his hands and against his lips made his mouth dry. He thought of seeing them in the daylight, seeing all of her, naked. It the sunshine and fired the coals of his imagination, and he deemed it only fair, for she'd seen him bathing in the river.

"I'll pull my bedroll and pillow by the fire today. Hopefully, they'll be dry enough to use tonight. I won't intrude into your bedroom again."

Fury built up in him, and he thought his head might explode. "Look at me and tell me you didn't enjoy what we did. I'm not that big a fool, Lily. I know when a woman is pretending, and I know when she's not. You weren't pretending. You were as anxious for it to happen as I was. Hell, you flew apart the minute I touched you."

Her head still bowed, she closed her eyes and muttered a shaky sigh.

"Now," he continued. "Look at me and tell me straight to my face that you didn't enjoy it."

Slowly, she raised her gaze to his. The hardness he saw there shocked him. "I didn't enjoy it. I might have needed it, Ross Benedict, but trust me, I'm not proud of it. And I didn't enjoy it."

He felt a stunning wash of angry frustration. "I don't believe you." He left her, eager to put her cold, calculated answer behind him.

An hour later, he was patching the roof when he heard a buggy rattle into the clearing. He spat a curse when he saw Trudy alight from the conveyance and make her way boldly to the cabin door.

Chapter Seven

L ily ushered Trudy into the kitchen and motioned to a chair. "I apologize for the mess. The roof leaked in here and I don't dare put anything away until it's mended." Lily poured her a cup of coffee, then turned back to the ginger cookie dough she was mixing.

"I've never been in Ross's cabin before," Trudy mused. "It's rather nice."

Cautiously surprised, Lily turned. "You haven't been here before?"

At Lily's expression, she added, "You don't believe me?"

Feeling foolish, Lily turned to her chore again. "I... I'm sorry. I guess... I just thought..."

"Well, you guessed, and you thought wrong. The only woman ever allowed in Ross's domain, until you came along, was Samantha, that snippy little sister of his."

Lily felt a warmth around her heart. "Oh, Samantha's not such a bad sort, Trudy. She's really quite charming and likable."

Trudy snorted. "Not to me, she isn't. Of course, I know why. She and the other ladies of Twin Hearts blame me for all the ills of the town."

Lily couldn't argue, so tried another tactic. "I thought it was very rude of Ross to bring you to the party last night."

She laughed. "Rude? Why?"

Lily rolled the cookie dough onto the flour covered counter, cut large circles of dough with the lid of a canning jar and slid them onto a baking sheet. "Surely he knew a kind of reception you'd get."

"Oh, he knew alright."

Lily removed the last loaf of bread from the oven, then slid in the cookies. "And it didn't bother you?"

Trudy shrugged. "I knew he had a reason for doing it the minute he asked me. He never invited me to one of his sister's parties before." She was quiet for a moment while she studied Lily. "I didn't know why he'd done it this time until I saw that you were there."

Lily's heart took a deep dip. "Why me?"

"Obviously, he wanted to make you jealous."

The comments stunned her, and she leaned against the counter. "Why on earth would you think that?" Damn! Why was her heart pounding so?

"I may not have an ounce of good sense when it comes to my own life, Lily, but I know, Ross. We've been...close for years. You've probably learned that what I do to keep body and soul together isn't the least bit respectable. Bluntly, I've allowed many of the men in this town to support me, Ross among them."

Lily's stomach clenched like a fist. Gritting her teeth, she continued to roll and cut cookies, pretending nothing was wrong. Foolish as it was, it bothered her that Ross and Trudy had slept together.

"But not too long ago, about the time I learned there was a beautiful red-haired widow cooking for the loggers, Ross came by for dinner. Sadly for me, that was all he wanted. He said it

78

wasn't me, that it was him. I knew then that someone had truly claimed his heart, and it was probably you."

"But...but," Lily sputtered. "We don't even like each other. We haven't. I mean, we didn't—"

"Don't, Lily. Whether you have or haven't doesn't matter. I just know that eventually you will. When I saw the way he watched you last night..." She sighed. "He didn't take his eyes off you. If he'd ever looked at me that way, I might have thought I really had a chance with him, but he never did," she added wistfully.

It was all Lily could do to continue working. Her hands shook. Her knees were weak. Her pulse roared through her head, humming in her ears. What Trudy said was nonsense. It was pointless to dwell on it anyway, for Ross had said himself that it wasn't natural for a man to be faithful.

"I'm sorry if what I said upset you, Lily."

Lily jumped at the sound of Trudy's voice. She'd all but forgotten she was there. "No," she said, shoring herself up. "It's not that really, it's just that I think you're reading something into this that isn't there."

"I see." She sounded disappointed. "Well, I guess I should go—"

"Wait," Lily interrupted. "Don't go. I appreciate your company, Trudy, and your candor. I'd like to help you."

"Help me?"

Lily sat in the chair across from her. "It's none of my business, and you can tell me so if you wish, but would you like to make your living another way?"

Clearly puzzled, Trudy stared at her. "Doing what? I'm not qualified to do anything gracious. I'm not even a very good cook."

Lily grasped her hand. "Oh, but everyone can cook. And what you don't know, I can teach you. I need help. Badly."

Trudy's face crumbled, and there were tears in her eyes. "You'd…you'd want *me* to work with you?"

Her expression left Lily feeling contrite. "I didn't mean to upset you. Really. It's none of my business what you do. And...and just because I wouldn't do it doesn't mean you shouldn't. I mean, I had no right to think you'd want to do something—"

"You would actually want me to work here with you? Really?"

"Sorry, I shouldn't have presumed."

Trudy put her face in her hands, sobbing quietly.

Lily felt awful. She went to the back of Trudy's chair and touched her shoulders. "I'm so sorry," she apologized again.

"I…can't believe you'd want me to work with you," Trudy stuttered between sobs. "You…you'd do that for me?"

Lily began to understand. "Of course. I asked you, didn't I?"

Trudy continued to cry. "No woman in this town has ever done anything nice for me before."

Lily bent and gave her a hug. "I'm not doing it just to be nice, Trudy. I really could use some help."

Truly grasped her arm but couldn't seem to stop crying. "Oh, Lily, thank you so much."

"What in the Hell's going on in here?"

Both women looked up as Ross entered the kitchen, but neither spoke.

"What did you say to her, Lily? Why in the hell did you make her cry?"

Fury at his assumption made her flush. "I didn't. I mean, I did, but it's not what you…" No, she would not defend herself. Not to him. "Oh, just shut up, Ross Benedict."

His gaze went to Trudy's tear-stained face. "Trudy? Did she upset you? Are you all right?"

Lily offered her a handkerchief, which she took and dabbed

at her eyes. Sniffing loudly, she answered, "Just shut up, Ross. Why do you always jump to conclusions? That's one of your worst habits."

He stood in the middle of the room, stunned by their verbal attacks. Throwing up his hands in defeat, he demanded, "Why in the hell are you mad at me?"

"Oh, just never you mind," Trudy answered, gaining control of herself. "If you must know, Lily offered me a job."

Russ appeared puzzled. "A job doing what?"

"Why helping her cook for the loggers, of course."

Lily saw the look of disbelief on his face before he quickly masked it. She knew what he was thinking: that she'd hired Trudy just to learn more about him. Oh, she thought, her fury mounting. He had an even bigger swelled head than she'd imagined.

"Trudy's going to cook." He sounded incredulous.

"I'm going to help, aren't I, Lily?"

"Of course," Lily answered, still standing behind Trudy. "And I do need some help, Ross. If you see Samantha before I do, tell her the job is just too much for one person. And with Maudie not able to help at all, I need someone. If she doesn't approve of what I've done, then perhaps she should find another cook." Suddenly Lily was angry with Samantha for the way she and all the other women in Twin Hearts had treated Trudy, and the men too, for that matter.

"You'd quit because of this?"

"Yes, Ross, I'd quit." She meant it, too. "In the meantime, I imagine you're hungry. There's some leftover stew on the back of the stove and eat the rest of those biscuits, please. I'd wait on you myself, but the way I'm feeling toward you and everyone else in this town right now, I'm afraid I'd dump the damn stew into your lap."

She hurried from the room, lifted her worn cape from the

chair by the fire, and sailed from the cabin, leaving Ross and Trudy alone in the kitchen.

Lily couldn't stay away for long because she just had too much work to do. And she felt better after her little explosion. Years ago, Jake had compared her temper to a volcano, erupting quickly and leaving destruction in its wake.

When she returned to the cabin, she was dismayed to find Trudy gone.

Ross was waiting for her in the kitchen. "Trudy pulled out the sheet of cookies from the oven before they burned."

In her haste to leave, Lily had forgotten them. She put them on a rack, then rolled and cut more, sliding them onto the sheet.

"So," he said behind her, "what little scheme have you cooked up?"

A coldness settled around her heart. "Scheme?"

"Yeah. Why in the hell would you hire Trudy?"

"And why shouldn't I?"

He snorted a laugh but didn't answer her.

She clutched the mixing spoon in her fist and turned on him. "If you think I hired her just to find out more about you, than you're even more arrogant than I'd imagined."

He snorted again. "Is that what you think?"

She shrugged. "I can think of no other reason you disapprove."

"The fact that she can't make a decent cup of coffee might have crossed your mind."

Lily felt her first niggle of uncertainty. "Why, surely she can cook. What woman can't?"

"Let's just say it's not one of her more...endearing attributes."

82

His innuendo angered Lily further. "Has it ever occurred to you that she might need a friend? She's had enough snickers and snubbings from the lot of you to last a lifetime, I have no doubt."

"I've never laughed at her, Lily."

"Perhaps not. But you did bring her to a party knowing full well that she wouldn't be welcome. That doesn't show much respect for her, do you think?"

He studied her quietly. "I'm sorry about that. It was a mistake. I shouldn't have put her in that position. But you do know what she does for a living, don't you?"

Suddenly tired of the game, she said, "Yes, I know. She told me herself. But I know where she's coming from. Ross. I've been there. I'm a widow too, remember? We're just different people. When I lost my husband, I'd already become quite independent, because, you see, he'd ceased to be part of my life at all. Of his own choosing. He found his...entertainment elsewhere, with good old-fashioned whores. And not just one, but many. I can't count the number of times he stumbled home reeking of some whore's cologne, expecting me to respond to—"

She stopped, angry that she'd revealed such a painful part of her life. "After he was killed, I had to do something to keep myself alive. I chose to cook because it was something I did well and enjoyed." She let that sink in before she parried on. "Obviously, Trudy knows what she does best. She enjoys the company of men in and out of her bed. But as I told you earlier, Ross Benedict, I might *need* that, but I certainly don't *enjoy* it." She was lying to herself as well as to him, for she *had* enjoyed it. Very, very much. She just wasn't proud of it.

He was quiet for a long, tense minute, his gaze never wavering from hers. "After what we did last night? Hell, there was a pleasure on both sides. Lily, don't—"

"Will you stop reminding me of that?" she pleaded. "I will tell you just one more time. I did not enjoy it."

Another minute stretched taut as a wire between them. Finally, he murmured, "I don't believe that's true for one goddamned minute."

She turned back to the counter, knowing his words held more truth than hers, but unwilling to admit it. "Believe what you wish. I can't stop you."

In an instant, he was behind her, pulling her against his chest. His hands cupped her breasts. His thumbs rubbed her nipples through her clothing. She felt him thick and hard against the small of her back, and every nerve in her body responded. Still, she fought it.

"Don't," she pleaded softly as one hand dipped below her waist, inching toward the juncture of her thighs. "Please, please don't." Even to her own ears, her request sounded feeble.

He turned her to face him, then bent to kiss her. She greeted him hungrily, without thought, for to think would make her crazy.

The kiss ignited their passion, and though Lily felt his fingers fumbling at the buttons of her dress, she couldn't have stopped him if she'd wanted to. His fingers on her bare breasts signaled the return of her sanity, and she pushed him away, her chest heaving.

"No." She held her bodice together, but he removed her hands tugging her clothes apart.

"It's only fair, Lily."

"What do you mean?" Desire hummed through her.

"You've seen me bare," he reminded her, though there wasn't a hint of humor in his eyes.

The memory of his naked body rose before her, rendering her weak with a hunger that dissolved her resistance. Desire and humiliation fought for control within her. She remembered his feelings about devotion and fidelity and her humiliation won. Shoving him away, she slumped into a chair and put her head on her arm, unable to keep from sobbing quietly. How could she continue this way? She wanted him. She needed him. She was falling head over heels in love with him. Ross Benedict, a man whom she could neither trust nor respect.

Remembering all the nights she spent alone, waiting in vain for Jake to return to her bed, she knew with a certainty that were she to succumb to her feelings for Ross, she would suffer the same pains all over again. God, why was her taste in men so pathetic?

Her suffering was like a knife to Ross's gut. He wanted to comfort her but knew she wouldn't allow it. And why should she? He remembered telling her that he couldn't—wouldn't—be faithful. How could he prove to her it had only been words? Words to keep himself from feeling things he didn't want to feel. Words to get her ire up so he could watch her bristle. Words that he'd always believed before, but that even then had suddenly sounded shallow and false. Words that made him sound exactly like the man she'd married and lost. Words that would separate them forever unless he could convince her he hadn't meant them.

He went to the door, bracing his arms on either side. "By the way," he said, remembering what he'd come in to tell her in the first place. "I checked up on Maudie. She's coming along fine, but the doctor wants to keep her for another week or so. I'm sorry, I meant to tell you earlier, but with Trudy here, I got kinda sidetracked."

Chapter Eight

While Ross finished patching up the holes in the cabin roof and the roof of Maudie's place, Lily moved her bedroll and pillow closer to the fire. She fully intended to sleep in it come bedtime. Occasionally she crossed her fingers, praying it would be dry.

Trudy returned later in the day to begin learning Lily's routine, but when evening rolled around, Lily and Ross were alone again.

They sat by the fire, Lily preparing menus and Ross reading a newspaper he'd picked up in town. Were anyone to look in, Lily realized, they would appear to be a couple spending a quiet evening together before going to bed.

Bed. Even the word caused her to feel flushed, for Ross's bed was no longer merely a place to sleep but also a place where she'd found complete satisfaction.

"I want to apologize."

His words came out of the blue, shaking her from her reverie. "I beg your pardon?"

"For starters, I want to apologize for shouting at you the day I came home from Chico and found you in my bedroom."

She allowed herself a small smile. "You mean the day I hit you in the head with the butt of your rifle?"

He made a gruff sound and cleared his throat. "Yeah, that's the day. I thought you and Sam were…conniving to…well, to get the two of us together," he finished, sounding embarrassed.

Lily had already discovered that was exactly what Sam had planned. However, she wanted to hear his side. "Why would you think such a thing?"

"Well, hell. She's been trying to marry me off for years. Every New Year's Eve, she pairs me up with one of her unmarried friends, and I spend the whole miserable evening feeling like bait on a stick. Last year, I decided I'd had it. I wasn't going to let her lead me around by the nose ever again, and I told her so. It was my New Year's resolution."

Clearing his throat once more, he folded the paper and put it on the table. "I thought maybe this was her way of getting back at me."

Lily tucked her feet under her and warmed them against her robe. "I can assure you I knew absolutely nothing of her plan, if indeed she had one."

"Oh, she had one, all right. She knew damned good and well that I wasn't going to be gone more than a few weeks. You probably thought the place wasn't occupied, because while I was gone, she'd had the cabin fumigated for fleas. She took all my clothes and the bedding too." He gave her a lopsided grin. "She rented you the place knowing it was occupied. By me. And that I'd be back just about the time you started to feel comfortable. I guess she thought we might…"

Her face void of expression, she asked, "She thought we might—what?"

"You know," he murmured. "Get together."

"Well," she managed to say, "I think we can assure her that

her plan failed. Miserably." She gave him a cold smile, then turned to her menu planning.

"Yeah," he reflected, rubbing his finger over his mustache. "The thing is, I just can't believe she's entirely wrong this time."

Lily's heart pounded hard beneath her robe. What he said was undoubtedly true. There had been something physical between them from the very beginning. There still was. And she might even wish things were different so it *could* be true, but he couldn't be trusted. He wasn't any better a man than Jake had been. Or her father. She'd rather have no man at all than one who couldn't be faithful.

"Physical attraction means nothing without fidelity, Ross," she said as her pulse thrummed at the base of her throat.

He frowned. "What in the hell is that supposed to mean?"

"It means," she began, her voice stern, "that Jake—my late husband—and I were quite compatible. Physically. But he was an unfaithful swine. I would sooner be celibate than be intimate with a man who cannot be faithful, no matter how much I'm attracted to him."

"Are you attracted to me, Lily?" His voice was as seductive as aged whiskey.

She squirmed, uncomfortable with his question. "I had certain needs the other night, and you…you were willing to slake them. That's all."

"Prove it."

"*What?*"

"Prove that's all it was, Lily. Prove you can kiss me without becoming aroused now that you're…slaked." Clearly amused, he began unbuttoning his shirt. His chest hair was so thick it poked through the buttonholes.

Lily's mouth went dry, but she was indignant just the same. "I'll do no such thing."

"Why not? Afraid you'll feel something?"

"Revulsion is what I'll feel," she snapped, having no intention of accommodating his ridiculous request. "Tell me," she asked, "do your other women actually like all that hair on your face?"

His dark eyes danced. "My other women? Are you admitting to being one of my women, Lily-love?"

"Oh, don't be foolish," she huffed, throwing her notebook on the floor. "And I'm not your love. I'm going to bed."

For a big man, he was surprisingly agile. He stopped her at the kitchen door and caught her to him, pressing her hands inside his shirt, against his warm flesh. "A hairy man can keep a woman warm, Lily."

She clenched her teeth against the urge to rub her face against his chest, but she couldn't control the pounding of her heart or the lush weakness in her lower abdomen. "Let me go."

"One kiss, Lily. One little kiss to prove that's all you need. That you don't want what we had last night. Now that you're *slaked*," he repeated, "one kiss should be easy enough to part with."

He was baiting her. Teasing her. So sure she couldn't resist him. Oh, how she hated arrogance in a man! She wanted in the worst way to watch him tumble from his lofty, self-centered perch.

"All right," she said. "It won't be a problem at all."

Raising up on her tiptoes, she touched his mouth. She expected him to grab her and devour her then she planned to stand limp and unresponsive.

He surprised her. She felt the tip of his tongue barely graze her lips, the flats of his thumbs circle her nipples, the front of his jeans press ever so lightly against her stomach.

Desire exploded like a bursting flower between her legs, and when his mouth opened over hers, she answered his kiss and threw her arms around his neck. Her self-control was gone.

Lifting her up, he wrapped her legs around his waist and pressed her buttocks with his hands, grinding against her. One hand snaked up beneath her gown and robe to her naked thigh, then to her bottom.

He stumbled with her to a chair, collapsing into it. She continued to straddle him, her desire so strong she flung all other thoughts aside as she reached for her pleasure. He opened her robe and unbuttoned her gown, freeing one breast. He kissed it. Licked the nipple. Nuzzled it with his beard, intensifying Lily's desire.

Her naked flesh pressed against the rigid fly of his jeans. She coaxed him to continue loving her breast while she rode him hard until the kernel of pleasure burst, sending her spiraling, rocking the world.

Her breath came hard, and felt boneless...and ashamed at her inability to control herself.

Drawing her hand to his fly, he unbuttoned it with his other hand and urged her to touch him. Desire flared again, but she fought it, pulling her hand away, refusing to be coaxed.

His hands spanned her thighs, his thumbs nudging her cleft. "Don't be cruel, Lily," he whispered, his voice husky as a raw wind.

She allowed him to return her hand to his fly, and she reached inside, against his drawers, finding him still thick and hard. Quivering with unwanted desire, she stroked him until he stiffened and shuddered beneath her.

"Ah, Lily-love, let's go to bed."

She scrambled off his lap, buttoning her nightgown as she hurried toward the kitchen. "Just because I serviced you doesn't mean I'll sleep with you."

She shut the door behind her, crossed to her bedroll, and fell up on it, angry tears stinging her eyes. She couldn't imagine what was wrong with her. She wanted him fiercely. She could love him easily. She probably already did. But he was all wrong for her. His kind was wrong for any woman who wanted a loving, faithful mate.

~

The next morning, Ross and his dog were nowhere around. Lily began working, and shortly after, Trudy arrived. They worked well together, and time passed quickly. When the clock on the mantel chimed eleven times, she heard the wagon from the camp stop out front. She and Trudy carried biscuits and apple fritters to the wagon, and she ordered the driver to retrieve the rabbit pies from the counter in the kitchen.

He returned with the meat pies and placed them in the wagon, his gaze raking Trudy. "Whatcha doing' here, Trudy?"

"I...I'm...um—"

She's working with me," Lily intervened.

He doubled over with laughter. "Working in a *kitchen*? Lost your way, did ya?"

Trudy actually blushed. "It's an honest living, Lou."

He wiped his eyes with his sleeve and tried to stop laughing. "Tell me it ain't nothing permanent, Trudy. The boys'll be disappointed if it is."

Lily pushed him toward the wagon. "Will you please get this food back to the camp before it gets too cold to eat?"

"Sure, sure," he murmured amicably. He hiked himself onto the wooden seat and snapped the reins over the team. But as he rode away, the women could still hear him laughing.

Lily put her arm around Trudy's waist. "Ignore him."

"This isn't going to be easy, Lily."

"Nothing worth having is come by easily, dear."

They went into the cabin, and Lily fixed lunch. "Have you ever considered marrying again?"

"There isn't a single man within miles. Except for Lou and a few of his cronies, and I don't like any of them. And, of course, there's Ross."

Lily's stomach pitched downward. "He...he never asked you?"

"No. At one time not too long ago, I really wanted him to, Lily."

"And...and now?"

"Now he's so crazy about you that no other woman matters."

Lily's feelings were all jumbled inside her. "Do you think there's a man alive who can be faithful to his wife?"

"Oh, yes," Trudy answered. "My Roy was."

"How did you know?"

"It's just one of those things I knew. We were so close. Not only was he my husband and my lover, he was my best friend. I could tell him anything."

Lily chewed on that, thinking about Jake. He'd been her husband and her lover, but her friend? She'd never thought of him that way. There were things about herself that she wouldn't have dared tell him.

They'd just sat down to eat when there was a knock at the door.

When Lily answered it, she gasped in surprise. "Donald!"

Donald South grinned his famous dimpled grin and hauled Lily into his arms, squeezing her tight. "You look good enough to eat, Lily-girl."

Lily allowed the embrace, then pulled away. "What on earth are you doing here?" Suddenly fear leapt into her chest. "And how did you find me?"

His hands stayed on her shoulders as he gazed at her. "You're beautiful as ever. Will you marry me?"

Lily tried to laugh, but his presence was so disturbing and surprising, she could only wonder if his employer wasn't far behind. She led him into the cabin. "You haven't changed an ounce. How did you find me?" she asked again.

"Wasn't hard," he answered. "I just kept going from town to town asking if a gorgeous redhead had moved in."

"We were just sitting down to lunch. Please, join us, Donald."

He hesitated. "I didn't know you had someone with you. I don't want to intrude."

"Nonsense." They entered the kitchen and Lily introduced him to Trudy, who actually blushed when he gallantly kissed her hand. Then she fixed lunch and set the table for three.

"Um, how are things at the estate?"

He gave her a knowing smile. "You mean, does the boss know I'm here?"

"So, you know what I did," she admitted.

"He was so mad he threw the empty cash box against the wall."

Lily felt her spine stiffen. "Well, he obviously wasn't going to pay me what he owed me, so I took it."

"And ran away like a thief in the night," Donald said.

Lily slumped. "He wasn't going to leave me alone, you know that, Donald."

Trudy cleared her throat. "I guess I should go."

Lily shook her head. "No need. In my previous employer's eyes, I'm a thief. There. I've said it but it isn't true. That money was mine."

93

Donald looked at the table. "He could make a case against you, Lily."

Shocked, she asked, "How?"

"He could say he was planning on paying you all along, but you stole from him before he had the chance."

"But he wasn't!"

"It would be your word against his, and he's mighty powerful in the community."

Lily narrowed her gaze at him. "So, he sent you to do his dirty work?"

Donald sighed. "He did. I was almost hoping I couldn't find you so he'd give up."

Lily swallowed the lump in her throat. "You still could," she suggested.

Donald chuckled. "I could, I guess. But I figured if you agreed to marry me, I could make this whole thing go away."

Reigning in her fear and disgust, Lily studied him. He was handsome, in a blond, Nordic kind of way. But suddenly she was frightened. This was her option?

"So, it's blackmail, is it?"

Donald gave her his most innocent smile. "I wouldn't think of it that way."

"But how else am I to think of it? I don't love you, Donald, and I will never marry again without love, no matter what the price."

He stood and looked down at her. "Don't be stupid."

Now she was furious. "Do your worst, if you must. Ride back to San Francisco and tell that bastard that he can put me in jail if he wants to, but I won't marry you just to get him off my back."

"I don't have to go that far, Lily."

Fear again took hold. "What do you mean?"

"He's in Chico."

"But that's just—"

"Yes. Just over those hills." He pointed east, toward the set of hills that separated them from civilization.

Suddenly Lily realized that she had known all along that that bastard would find her in the end.

She was tired of hiding. "Then do your worst, Donald. I'm no coward. I'm done running."

He looked at her and shook his head. "I'm sorry it has come to this, Lily, I really thought you had some sense."

Sure, she thought, after he'd just called her stupid.

"Just leave," she said. "I'll be here."

"Just whose cabin is this?" he asked.

"It's mine," came the gruff answer.

Everyone turned toward the door. Lily's jaw dropped when she saw Ross.

He stepped into the kitchen, his dark eyes holding not one ounce of pleasure as they examined Donald South.

"I can't believe it." Trudy's voice was filled with the same disbelief Lily felt. "You've shaved off your beard *and* your mustache."

Lily couldn't believe it either. She was weak and puzzled and filled with longing at the sight of him. He was as handsome as his sister was beautiful. His cheekbones were high, his lips just wide enough to be sensual, and why she'd never noticed the thick, curly lashes that rimmed his eyes before now, she'd never know. His hair had been trimmed and capped his head in deep, coffee-brown waves.

"It's only hair," he answered tersely. "It'll grow back." His gaze still hadn't wavered from Donald's.

Donald stood, a wary expression on his face. "And you are…"

"My name isn't important. It sounds to me like you're threatening this woman. Is that true?"

95

Appearing to bolster himself up, Donald stood tall. "She stole money from my employer."

"I did not!" Lily shouted. "That money was due me."

"And you couldn't have waited until he paid you?"

Frustrated and angry, Lily said, "You know very well he wasn't going to pay me."

Before Donald could respond, Ross announced, "You go tell your employer that if he has issues with this woman, he can come to me."

Lily gave him an odd look but didn't speak.

Donald looked at Lily, then back at Ross. "You? What have you got to do with this?"

"She's my fiancé."

Lily was gobsmacked. What was he up to?

Donald threw Lily a menacing glance. "And you couldn't tell me this?"

"She doesn't need to answer to you or anyone else. Now, if you don't leave my property right now, I'll show you out personally, and it won't be politely."

Donald picked up his hat and went to the door. "This isn't over, Lily." After Donald left, Lily just stared at Ross. Finally, she whispered, "Why would you say such a thing."

Ross shrugged. "It got him out of here, didn't it?"

Lily turned as Trudy said, her voice still filled with wonder, "Well, it's time for me to get along home."

Regaining her composure, Lily said, "Come back tomorrow. There will be plenty to do."

Trudy merely nodded, shook her head and left them alone.

Lily fussed with the pots Trudy had washed, stacking them neatly on the shelf near the window. "But it won't be the end of it. Donald's boss could have me put in jail for theft."

"We can deal with that if and when the time comes."

Lily tried to sound flippant. "By carrying on your charade?"

He raked his fingers through his newly cut hair. "It doesn't have to be." Lily could hardly breath. "What?"

"You heard me."

She couldn't grapple with this right now. It was too sudden and so terribly ridiculous. "I hope you didn't shave for my sake Ross."

"Are you trying to avoid the subject?"

She wiped off the table, her hands shaking. "Is there really a subject, Ross?"

"Marry me, Lily."

Her heart took flight, nearly breaking free from her chest. "I...I...I...can't do that."

"Why in hell not?"

Finally able to gather the ragged edges of her feelings and bring herself back under control, she answered, "Why should I marry you, Ross? I...I'd always thought I'd marry once in life, for love. Even before Jake died, that foolish illusion was shattered. Jake wasn't a faithful husband. I won't marry another man who isn't."

Slumping into a chair, he rubbed his fingers over his smooth skin, then dug the heels of his palms into his eyes. "Damnit. What makes you think I wouldn't be faithful?"

"Because you told me as much." When he started to interrupt, she put her fingers against his mouth. "You told me it wasn't natural for a man to be faithful to just one woman."

He enclosed her fingers in his and held them. "Do you love me, Lily?"

She tried to tug her fingers away, but he pulled her onto his lap. "I might, but...but that isn't reason enough to marry you."

"What if I told you I loved you too?"

Her heart zinged with hope again, but she cautioned herself against it. "It...it still wouldn't be enough, Ross. Love without trust isn't enough."

"*Damnit*. I'm not your bloody Jake!"

"But that day when I was washing your bedding, you sounded just like him."

"I was trying to get a rise out of you, that's all."

"You did. And I'll never forget it." She pushed herself off his lap.

He stood, his hands in his back pockets. "What can I do to change your mind?"

"At this point, nothing," she answered, fighting tears. She couldn't succumb. She just couldn't. But marriage to Ross beckoned, for she knew it would be a heady, satisfying, fulfilling life—if he didn't feel the need to stray.

Chapter Nine

Ross stormed from the cabin, went to the shed and grabbed the ax and the scythe, then strode angrily toward the brush he should have cleared weeks before.

Every time he'd ever spouted off about a man's inability to be faithful to a woman, it had come back to haunt him. There was no way in hell he could convince Lily he would be faithful. But that wasn't going to stop him trying, damnit. The very thought of someone coming along and taking her away from him ate at him like acid. Never before had he cared enough about a woman to want her for his own. He wanted Lily and only Lily. He knew he wanted to spend the rest of his life with her. And he'd deal with that bastard Donald what-ever-his-name-was once and for all.

He loved Lily. He loved her for befriending Trudy when no one else would. He loved her wit and even her sharp tongue, for he knew that beneath it all, she was vibrant and passionate. The idea that she would be even more fervent if she trusted him made him weak. He sat down on the tree stump and scratched

Red's ears. "What has she done to me, boy?" Red leaned against him, begging for more.

Paying little attention to his menial task, he imagined all the places he wanted to make love to her. In the river, with her legs wrapped around his waist; on the floor in front of the fire, with her astride, outside on a bed of leaves in front of God and the world.

Suddenly he heard a crashing noise, and the next thing he knew, he was on the ground...

Lily heard him scream and Red barked furiously. Terror reached into her throat, and she instinctively grabbed Ross's rifle, fled from the cabin, and ran toward the noise. She faltered, only briefly, when she saw Ross on the ground, grappling with a black bear, Red attempting to divert the bear's interest.

Raising the rifle, she shot it into the air, praying the noise would scare the animal off. At the sound of the gunshot, the bear released Ross, lifting her head long enough for Ross to roll away and scramble to his knees. Lily shot again, and the bear lumbered off into the brush.

She flung the rifle to the ground and rushed to Ross. He was still on his knees, blood dripping from his chest and forearms.

"Oh, Ross! Oh, dear God!" She grabbed him under one arm and helped him to his feet.

"I was...thinking about you," he mumbled. "Not...not paying attention—"

"Hush," she soothed, trying to be strong though she felt so weak. "Come on, now. Help me get you to the cabin."

They struggled to the porch, where Ross had difficulty making it up the steps. "Chest...like fire and...and raw blisters."

He stumbled inside, and she could barely keep him from slipping to the floor. "Oh, my poor dear, just a little farther, darling. Just a little farther."

It seemed like an hour before they got to the bed, but once there, she willed her hands to stop shaking and examined his wounds. A wave of fear coated her stomach.

Sidestepping an anxious dog, she rushed to the kitchen, grabbed the teakettle, some dish towels, and her darning kit. Once back at his side, she cut his shirt away and dabbed at the wounds, cringing at the appearance of the ragged flesh.

His face was pinched with pain, but he grabbed her fingers and brought them to his lips. "You...you called me dear. Darling."

A blush stole into her cheeks. "Don't talk, Ross. Save your strength, please."

"I...I would be...faithful, Lily. I knew...the minute I saw you that..." He coughed, gasping against his pain. "...that I'd never want another woman."

Tears welled up in her eyes and slid down her cheeks. "Shhh," she whispered, working at a frantic pace to clean his wounds.

She heard the sound of horses outside, and in a moment, Sam was beside her.

"Oh, my god," she whispered, her mouth quivering. "What happened?"

Lily continued to dab at his wounds, for they still bled. "He must have somehow gotten too close to a black bear's den. She attacked him." She turned to Sam. "He needs help, Sam. Go. Please. Bring a doctor."

Sam hadn't taken her eyes off her brother. She backed away, toward the door. "The...the doctor is over at the camp right now. I...I just came from there."

"Please, Sam. Hurry."

Sam rushed out, and Lily prayed she'd return with the doctor before Ross bled to death.

~

Sam walked the doctor out, then returned to the beside. Lily sat slumped in a chair by the bed.

"He'll be all right, don't you think?"

Lily rubbed her eyes. "He's lost a lot of blood, but the doctor seemed to think he would."

Sam sat on the edge of the bed, her fingers touching Ross's cheek. "He shaved his beard and his mustache. I'd forgotten how handsome he is."

Lily could only nod quietly. She remembered her harsh words and his softer, seductive ones: *"A hairy man can keep a woman warm, Lily."*

There was a sudden catch in her throat, and she felt a wealth of tears press against the back of her eyes. Oh, why had she been so nasty? If he should…should die, he'd never know how she really felt about him.

"That's funny," Sam said wistfully.

"What?"

"It's odd that he would shave. He's been proud of his beard for years."

"Perhaps…he was just tired of it."

"I don't think so."

"Why not?"

She gave Lily a little smile and shrugged. "Last New Year's Eve, I teased because his date—a woman I forced him into asking to my party—complained about all his facial hair. We made a wager." She pulled a handkerchief from her dress pocket and blew her nose. "I bet him that he'd shave off his beard and mustache if he met the right woman and she asked

102

him to."

Lily's heart expanded and she felt so much love for Ross, mingled with shame at how she'd spoken to him, that she had to turn away.

"I didn't ask him to do it, Sam."

Sam continued to watch her brother. "Maybe you're right. He probably just got tired of it."

Lily gave her a wobbly smile and shook her head. "No."

"What?"

"I...I didn't ask him to shave, but I did tell him I didn't like his beard." She swallowed the lump in her throat. "He asked me to marry him, Sam."

Sam gasped and brought her hands to her mouth. "He did? And what did you say, Lily, what did you say?"

Lily's tears came freely now, and she hunted for her own handkerchief. Unable to find it, she brought her apron to her face and wiped her eyes. "I told him I wouldn't marry a man I couldn't trust."

At Sam's crestfallen look, she added, "He'd admitted to me that it wasn't normal for a man to stay faithful to one woman. My late husband was like that, Sam. No matter how much I love Ross, I can't bear the thought of him being with someone else. I guess I'm just selfish that way."

The clock on the mantel chimed five times.

"Oh, dear. I have to pick up Derek at the camp." Sam stood. As she swung her cape over her shoulders, she studied Lily. "Will you be all right here alone?"

Lily gave her a reassuring smile. "Of course. Go. Take care of your husband."

"I'll come back in the morning." Fresh tears spilled down Sam's cheeks. "Oh, Lily...I'd so wished the two of you..." She pressed her hand over her mouth and ran from the room.

Once Sam was gone, Lily turned her gaze on Ross. The

doctor had given him something to kill the pain and help him rest. He was asleep. Red had jumped onto the bed and was curled up at Ross's side. Lily left him there.

She sat on the edge of the bed and studied him. Had he really shaved for her? Did she dare believe that he really loved her enough to be faithful?

~

Lily watched him into the night. She soothed his face with a cool, damp cloth. She checked his bandages to make sure he wasn't bleeding.

If he'd been thinking about her when he was attacked, then, it was her fault. Tears stung her eyes again, and she swiped them away with her sleeve.

They'd gotten off on the wrong foot, that much she knew. And all because sweet, meddlesome little Samantha had wanted a wife for her brother.

Lily wiped his face again, letting her fingers linger on his skin. His beard was already a rough stubble. She bent and kissed his forehead, nose, his mouth, his chin.

She sat back and rubbed her shoulders. She was tired, but she couldn't leave him. She continued to watch him, her mouth curving into a shy smile.

She left him just long enough to bank the fire, then hurried to the kitchen and grabbed her nightgown. Back in the bedroom, she undressed and slipped into her gown, turned down the lamp, and slid into the bed beside him, careful not to lean against his bandaged forearms. She justified her actions by telling herself that if he woke up, she'd know it.

She dozed lightly, in tune with his every movement and the changes in his breathing. Toward morning, however, she fell into a deeper sleep.

Awakening with a start, she opened her eyes and found herself looking into his. They were warm as fresh-brewed coffee.

"I'd like to wake up this way every morning, Lily-love," he said with a drowsy smile.

She swallowed the emotion that swelled in her chest, threatening to erupt into her throat. "I...thought it best to be close, just in case you needed me." She attempted to scoot to the other side of the bed and get out, but he tugged her back.

"Don't go."

Without an argument, she settled next to him, then hiked herself up on her elbow. "How do you feel this morning?"

He grinned, sporting a deep, lovely dimple in his left cheek. Lily's self-control was slipping fast. "Like I've been attacked by a bear."

She let out a shaky breath. "Ross, you could have been killed."

He continued to smile at her. "Would you have grieved for me, Lily-love?"

She gave him a gentle smack on the shoulder. "Don't tease about this."

"But would you have?"

She bent and kissed him, thrilling as his mouth responded. "Yes," she admitted. "I would have grieved for the rest of my life."

"Do you love me, Lily?"

She returned his smile. "Yes," she answered simply.

"Will you marry me?"

She wasn't even tempted to ask if he'd be faithful; somehow, she just knew he would. "I guess I'd better. There are too many women out there who would take my place in a minute."

He was suddenly serious. "There's not another woman alive who could ever take your place, Lily."

She kissed him again, careful not to touch any of his numerous bandages. "Samantha will be delighted that her plan worked."

He stroked her hair. "Samantha deserves a good spanking. I'll have to talk to Derek about that."

Lily chuckled. "Be careful, she just might enjoy it."

He laughed out loud, then coughed and groaned. "Why, Lily Sawyer, I'm surprised at you."

She snuggled against him briefly. "Life is full of surprises, darling."

With a clumsy motion, he reached over and touched her breast. "I can't wait."

Warmth spread through her at his touch, but she forced herself to get out of bed. "The doctor and Sam will both be here soon. Trudy, too, I suspect. It wouldn't do for them to catch us in bed together."

"It would just force me to make an honest woman of you."

As she unbuttoned her nightgown, she said, "You'll do that anyway once you've healed properly." She picked up her clothes and walked toward the door.

"Lily?"

Turning, she smiled at him. "Yes?"

"Dress in here." His gaze was hot, his request bold.

Pausing only briefly, she put her clothes on the chair by the bed and pulled her nightgown off over her head. The room was cold; her nipples tightened immediately.

His gaze was almost reverent. "Pink nipples. My favorite kind," he added with a smile.

She blushed, feeling the heat from the roots of her hair to her womanhood. "Seen enough, you dirty old man?" she asked, her voice soft and loving despite the harsh words.

His gaze raked her, settling on the thatch of hair between

her legs. "Red. My favorite color." He held out his hand. "Come here."

She moved toward him. "Ross, someone will be here any minute—" She gasped as his fingers touched her, then felt her knees go weak when he slid a finger inside. With all her strength, she pulled away, and started to dress, noting the tent over his groin.

"One day soon, I'm going to make love to you and watch you when you come, Lily. If I'm not too far gone myself."

His words intensified his hunger, but she forced herself to finish dressing, surprisingly comfortable having him watch her. "I'll make you some oatmeal before I start cooking for the crew." She crossed to the door.

"Lily?"

She stopped, her hand on the latch. "Yes?"

"I love you," he said simply. "The bedroom is ours."

With tears of joy in her eyes, she hurried form the room, allowing his words to nudge her heart. It opened like a flower, and Lily knew she'd found her future husband, her lover, and her friend. She also knew they would be together until the end of time.

Epilogue

News Year's Eve, 1880

From across the room, Ross watched as Lily sat on the sofa to visit with a recuperating Maudie. Red had taken a special liking to the old woman and was often by her side, as if instinctively knowing she needed watching. He was curled up at her feet right now. Under Lily's care, the old woman had done remarkably well and was still able to live independently in the tiny cabin attached to theirs.

And strangely, that damn cat of hers sensed something was different about Lily, and stayed close even after she had a litter of kittens, for which they found loving homes.

Ross's heart swelled with love and pride every time he looked at Lily. He couldn't believe she was really his wife. Who would have thought that love could do such things to a man? Last year at this time, he'd been completely unaware of the power of love, easily spouting platitudes about infidelity, strutting around like an arrogant rooster. Then Lily entered his life, and all that changed.

They had traveled to meet with her former employer to settle the issue together. When the bastard appraised an angry Ross, he backed down with little encouragement.

Ross was pouring himself another glass of applejack when an obviously pregnant Samantha sidled up to him.

"Kind of a different party than the one we had last year, isn't it?" Her eyes were filled with merriment.

He gave her a half smile. "I was thinking the same thing."

"You lost the bet, you know," she reminded him.

He tweaked her nose. "One bet I was happy to lose, Sam."

"Are you going to thank me for meddling?"

"You deserve to be spanked," he said with a growl. "You can't just throw two people together and expect them to fall in love."

"But I did, didn't I?" She gave him an innocent smile.

"That was dumb luck," he answered.

She sighed. "Maybe, but you are happy, aren't you, Ross?"

His smile broadened. "Yeah, Sam, I'm happy as hell."

She sighed again, sounding contented as she studied Lily. "Lily looks...different."

Ross cleared his throat. "She looks beautiful as always."

"No," Sam answered with a shake of her head. "She sort of glows." With a tiny gasp, she grabbed his arm. "She's pregnant, isn't she?"

Ross wasn't sure how to answer. Lily had gotten pregnant the very first night they'd been together, which was a full six weeks before they got married. They'd hoped to keep it a secret awhile longer.

Sam tugged at his sleeve. "She is, isn't she?"

"Yeah, she is."

She studied him. "Aren't you happy about it?"

"I'm so happy I could crow, but don't advertise it." And he was. He couldn't wait to start a family with this woman who had so completely stolen his heart.

"Why not? What's the big secret?"

He shrugged. "We just want to...to wait awhile before we announce it."

"Uh-h, the famous Benedict telltale mid-sentence hesitation. Why Ross Benedict. I do believe you're not telling me the entire truth. When is the baby expected?"

Lily appeared beside them. "The baby is due in early July," Lily answered, offering Sam a patient smile.

Samantha pulled her close and gave her a hug, which she returned.

"July?" Sam counted on her fingers, then looked at the two of them, her mouth open in surprise. "What, that would mean—"

"That would mean, Samantha Mae," Ross interrupted, "that whatever you're thinking, you'd better keep it to yourself."

She grinned, her smile nearly splitting her mouth. "So, I wasn't wrong about you two after all. Oh, Lily! Our babies will be so close in age, they'll be playmates." Her eyes filled with happy tears. "Isn't that wonderful?"

"Yes, Sam, it's wonderful. And darling," Lily added, giving Ross a squeeze, "Sam actually deserves all the credit for bringing us together, don't you think?"

Ross chuckled. "We can't deny it. We can return the favor by naming our first child after her."

Sam's smile wobbled. "Why, that's so sweet, Ross. Thank you. I'd be honored."

"Yeah," Ross said, "Samantha the Snoop, or Meddlesome Mae. Which do you prefer?"

She gave him a mock insulted look, then swept graciously

into the waiting arms of her husband. "Ross is picking on me, Derek, darling."

Derek kissed her full on the mouth, then asked, "Shall I give him a sound thrashing, my love?"

She snuggled against his chest, tossing Ross a devilish look over her shoulder as Derek whisked her away. "I think someone should."

"We do owe her a lot, Ross."

"I know, but it wouldn't do to let her know how much we really appreciate it. She'll be a doting aunt as it is."

Lily rested her head against her husband's shoulder. "And I don't imagine you'll be a doting uncle at all."

"Oh, I fully intend to be. But," he said, bending to kiss her, "I'll be an even more doting father."

Lily closed her eyes, wonder filling her. "I never believed I could be this happy."

For a brief moment, Ross remembered the New Year's resolution he'd made the year before, vowing never to let Samantha meddle in his life again. He pulled Lily close, loving how she felt in his arms. Hell, everyone knew that New Year's resolutions were made to be broken.

Don't miss out on your next favorite book!

Join the Satin Romance mailing list
www.satinromance.com/mail.html

THANK YOU FOR READING

∼

Did you enjoy this book?

We invite you to leave a review at your favorite book site, such as Goodreads, Amazon, Barnes & Noble, etc.

DID YOU KNOW THAT LEAVING A REVIEW...

- Helps other readers find books they may enjoy.
- Gives you a chance to let your voice be heard.
- Gives authors recognition for their hard work.
- Doesn't have to be long. A sentence or two about why you liked the book will do.

About the Author

Jane's first historical romance, *Secrets of a Midnight Moon*, was heralded as 'sensitive and sensuous, violent and tender.'

"I found the plot to my first novel in a little known history of Northern California Indians when I learned that Native Americans were being taken as slaves by the settlers, their families threatened with death and dismemberment if they tried to leave. Yes, one can weave a romance around such an appalling event!"

Since then she has published fifteen full length novels and four anthologies, all dealing with the perils and passions of romantic historical fiction.

She graduated from the University of Minnesota majoring in American and Russian History revealing that, "while all of my stories are set in the US, I had hoped one day to set one in Russia, though in my opinion, the best ones have already been written."

Jane continues to write and also edits for Melange Books. She currently lives in St. Paul, Minnesota with her husband, Richard Noer.

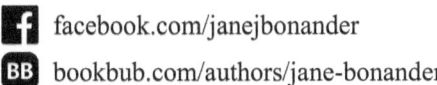

facebook.com/janejbonander

bookbub.com/authors/jane-bonander

www.ingramcontent.com/pod-product-compliance
Lightning Source LLC
Chambersburg PA
CBHW050830180626
46814CB00004B/1543